About th

Sibel Hodge is the author of bestselling romantic comedy *Fourteen Days Later*. She has 8 cats and 1 husband. In her spare time, she's Wonder Woman! When she's not out saving the world from dastardly demons, she writes books for adults and children.

Her work has been shortlisted for the Harry Bowling Prize 2008, Highly Commended by the Yeovil Literary Prize 2009, Runner up in the Chapter One Promotions Novel Comp 2009, nominated Best Novel with Romantic Elements in 2010 by The Romance Reviews, and a Finalist in the eFestival of Words 2013. Her novella *Trafficked: The Diary of a Sex Slave* has been listed as one of the Top 40 Books About Human Rights by Accredited Online Colleges. For more information, please visit www.sibelhodge.com

Praise for the
AMBER FOX MYSTERIES:

"If you like Janet Evanovich's Stephanie Plum I think you will really like Amber Fox - I know I do." ~ Martha's Bookshelf

"Amber Fox is a modern, career-driven woman who seems to be a cross between Kinsey Milhone and Gracie Hart (Miss Congeniality). I enjoyed the great mixture of action adventure and slapstick. I found myself chuckling out loud and on one occasion snorting water out my nose." ~ Coffee Time Romance & More

"Amber Fox was hilarious with her tough as nails outer persona and her hysterical one-liners that were frequently laugh out loud funny. I definately recommend picking this book up!!" ~ The Caffeinated Diva reads...

"Amber Fox is the kind of strong lead female character with a great sarcastic wit that I love to read." ~ To Read, Perchance to Dream

Also by Sibel Hodge

Fiction:
Fashion, Lies, and Murder (Amber Fox Mystery 1)
Money, Lies, and Murder (Amber Fox Mystery 2)
Voodoo, Lies, and Murder (Amber Fox Mystery 3)
Trafficked: The Diary of a Sex Slave
The See-Through Leopard
Fourteen Days Later
My Perfect Wedding
The Baby Trap
How to Dump Your Boyfriend in the Men's Room
(and other short stories)
It's a Catastrophe

Non Fiction:
A Gluten Free Taste of Turkey
A Gluten Free Soup Opera
Healing Meditations for Surviving Grief and Loss

"If I must die, let it be death by chocolate"

Chapter 1

Life was good. For once, I was having no men dramas—I mention "dramas", plural, because for a long time there'd been two men in my life. Now I'd finally made a decision about them, and I was back with Brad. For good this time. OK, it's a long story; here's the short version. Brad was my ex-fiancé, who became my boss, then my fiancé again. Romeo had been my boyfriend in between the Brad saga and was a lovely guy. It's just that Brad had stopped at nothing to get me back and to be honest, he was my soul mate. See, simple! Or not. Which was why I'd been having said men dramas. But not anymore. I wasn't stressed about men now and was ecstatically happy with Brad. In fact, we were flying off to Vegas in seven days to get married. Yay! Plus, in my job as an insurance investigator for Hi-Tec Insurance, owned by Brad, no one had tried to kill me lately, which seemed to happen a lot. Somehow, I always seemed to become embroiled in cases where the bad guys wanted to shut me up. I mean, I admit I have a big mouth and I'm not afraid to use it, but the whole kill Amber thing was getting a tad repetitious. And, as an extra bonus, I'd just picked up some rather large slices of mocha choca cake for breakfast. Scrumalicious. Coffee, chocolate, *and* cake, three of my favourite things all rolled into one. So, actually, life wasn't just good, it was pretty much perfect.

I wandered through the front doors of the plush Hi-Tec Insurance office with a happy smile, humming to myself as I walked past the empty reception and salivating at the prospect of the cake. All I had to do this week before we got married was tie up some loose ends on the case files I'd been working, buy some sexy undies for the wedding night, have a bikini wax, and get a manicure. Easy peasy. I was thinking pink glitter (for the manicure, not the bikini wax), or maybe something like Hot Vixen, just because I loved the name on the bottle. I could picture myself being a Hot Vixen on our honeymoon. Elvis and the Chapel of Love took care of the rest of the nuptials, so it was going to be a lovely, relaxing week for once and nothing could possibly go wrong before the big day.

I was loaded with four slices of cake to share with Tia, the receptionist, and some bizarre, soggy-looking tofu concoctions for Brad and Hacker, who were both into the health food thing.

I entered the office I shared with Hacker. Tia sat next to him. They both stared at me with a worried expression.

'What? Have I got lipstick on my teeth or something?' I ran a finger around my mouth. 'Or is it my hair?' My curly waves had a mind of their own and often bordered on a scary Krusty the Clown look, although I'd had a trim for the wedding after a nasty incident of hair singeing, so it couldn't look that bad. Plus I'd poured practically a whole bottle of argan oil conditioning serum over it.

Hacker and Tia gave each other a sheepish glance before letting out a nervous laugh.

I eyed them suspiciously, my investigator-ish intuition shifting up a notch. To avoid my gaze, Hacker, the office tech guru, suddenly found his massive bank of computer monitors and electrical equipment very interesting. I'd yet to see a computer system he couldn't break into. Originally from Haiti, he'd been in the SAS with Brad. He was six foot six and the spitting image of the rapper Snoop Dogg. He had two plaits that stuck up in the air like antennas, a gold front tooth, and a penchant for wearing various gangsta rapper hoodies. Today he wore one that said "Keep Calm and Rap". His real name was Roderick, but I seriously doubted anyone who'd ever called him that lived to tell the tale. Tia was American and had a heart-shaped face, blonde ringlets, and big blue eyes. But don't let the ditzy blonde act fool you. She was a tough little thing. Tia liked to dress loud with a capital *L*. Today she wore a tie-dye maxi dress of psychedelic colours you could see from outer space. She probably made those people who monitored the orbiting satellites reach for their sunglasses. Tia and Hacker had been seeing each other for a while, so maybe I'd just caught them in the middle of a raunchy discussion about their sex life.

Under my scrutinizing gaze, Tia let out her signature snorty giggle, which sounded like a hyena on crack.

'OK, what's up with you two?' I asked, handing out the food.

They glanced at each other again before saying, 'Nothing' in unison.

'Hmm.' I raised a disbelieving eyebrow and opened up the box of cake. A pre-appreciation dribble came on as I lifted the delicious mixture to my lips. In full drooling mode, I noticed a woman in Brad's office across the corridor.

My hand froze mere millimetres from my face as I took in the scene through the glass window. The woman sat on his desk, facing Brad and away from us. Yes, actually on his desk. And if that wasn't a bit too familiar for my liking, her face was up close to his ear. She whispered something before tossing her long, highlighted hair over her shoulder and giggling. Then she reached out, ran her fingers along the side of his neck, and walked them down his chest. The touch was not in an 'I'm just a friend' way, either. Oh, no. This little stroke was more of an 'I want to get you into bed' kind of way. Through Brad's slightly open door, I could hear their murmured voices but couldn't make out what they were saying.

My appetite vanished. A hot, bubbling sensation erupted in my stomach. I think I might've even let out a growl.

I put the cake back on my desk. Now I knew what Tia and Hacker had been staring at when I came in, and it wasn't me. It was that…that woman behind me.

'OK, spill,' I whispered to them. 'Who's that? And why's she practically molesting Brad?' I jerked my head in the direction of Brad's office.

'Er…' Tia's eyes widened, looking like she was panicking about giving me some potentially bad news.

'Spit it out,' I said.

'It's Aleesha,' Hacker said.

I frowned. The name wasn't ringing any clangers.

'Aleesha who?'

He shrugged. 'You know, that glamour model. She just calls herself "Aleesha".'

My eyes narrowed as I glanced back at the woman, who now fondled Brad's ear. My temperature shot up a few degrees in recognition. 'That slutty woman who's always in the paper for wearing skirts that could double as belts, and getting out of cabs flashing off the fact she's wearing no knickers?' My mouth contracted into a thin line.

'That's the one.' Tia pulled a worried face.

'And what's she doing with Brad?' I asked, although maybe I already knew the answer. By the look of things, she'd have her man-hungry claws into him quicker than I could say 'trailer trash'. She'd had more husbands and fiancés than I'd had junk food, which was saying something. Every week she was plastered over the tabloids and celebrity magazines with a new man, or because of some drunken exploit, or she'd decided to dish the dirt on an ex.

'She's a client.' Tia nibbled on the edge of her cake.

'What's she got insured with us? Her double FFs?' I spat out.

'She's also Brad's ex-girlfriend,' Hacker said.

My jaw flew open. 'What? When? I didn't know about that.' Ew. The thought of them together was just ick.

'It was about a year ago, when you'd broken up.' Hacker tucked into his tofu mess to avoid my searing gaze. 'It didn't last long,' he added, as if that was supposed to make me feel better somehow.

Tia leaned in towards me. 'Apparently, someone's

stalking her, and she wants Brad to look into it for her.'

I exhaled loud enough to be heard in Russia. 'This is an insurance company. What's stalking got to do with insurance?' I asked, more to myself than anyone. 'Nothing.' I answered myself, too.

'Well, she's got life insurance with us.' Tia shrugged. 'Maybe he's looking into it as a favour to her. Since they used to date and stuff.'

I glared at Brad and Aleesha again. I couldn't see her hand now. Where the hell was it?

Brad looked up at that moment, his grey-blue eyes widening as he registered my look of disapproval. Or maybe it was because my face had probably turned an angry shade of Hot Vixen red like I was about to have a stroke. He shook his head slightly at me, and I could feel another growl coming on.

I wasn't usually a jealous kind of girl. No, seriously. OK, maybe just a smidgen. It's just that Aleesha was...well, how can I put it politely...a slapper. One of her specialties was being a home-wrecker, splitting up couples and then dumping the men when she got bored of them and moving onto the next one. What if she thought she had unfinished business with Brad? What if she wanted to get him back? What if—

Uh oh. The 'what ifs' are starting again!

I was queen of 'what ifs'. It was part of the problem why it had taken me so long to get back with Brad the second time around. Yes, I admit it; I had a neurotic side, too. Well, I am only human.

'Amber, can you come into my office, please,' Brad called out to me.

I took a deep breath, plastered a smile on my face,

and walked across the hallway. Knowing what a self-centered woman Aleesha was, no way I was going to let her see she was bothering me. Nuh-uh.

I pushed the door open wider and leaned against the frame, looking to see where her hand was.

Brad lifted her hand from somewhere under the table and stood up. 'Aleesha, I'd like you to meet Amber, my investigator. She's very qualified to help sort this matter out for you.'

Investigator? Hello! And your fiancée!

Aleesha rose from the desk and positioned herself next to Brad, eyeing me like a potential challenge, draping one arm possessively round his shoulder.

Get off his shoulder! That's my shoulder.

Before I could say something, Brad removed her arm. A slight frown of what I took to be distaste appeared on his otherwise usual poker face.

Aleesha changed her hair colour like the weather. This week it was chocolate brown with caramel streaks. She had enough makeup on to keep L'Oréal in business for a whole year, pouty lip implants, and fake nails. In fact, most of her was fake, including the boobs. Nothing that defied the laws of gravity like that could possibly be real. Still, at least if she was ever drowning at sea, they'd provide an excellent buoyancy aid. Not that I was feeling inferior in the boobage area, you understand. I mean, I have a nice pair of C Cups, and anything more than a handful is a waste, quite honestly.

I fantasized that maybe she was really wearing a wig and was completely bald underneath all that hair, but that was just wishful thinking. The hair was probably one of the few parts that were real. Her long legs were practically skinnier than my arms, and in her shrink-wrapped leather trousers, she didn't just have a camel toe going on, she had the whole hoof. She wore a skin-tight turquoise sun top, despite the freezing UK day. Good luck getting that gear off in a hurry. On her wrist, a gold bracelet with a charm of the Eiffel Tower and a camera swung around as she stroked Brad's shoulder.

I folded my arms, and my fake smile got wider. 'And what can I do for you both today?' Bother me? Nah. OK, OK, maybe just a smidgen.

'Aleesha has a bit of a problem that she wants us to sort out.' Brad sat down again.

I raised an eyebrow. *Really? Only one?*

Aleesha sat down in the chair opposite Brad, crossing one leg over the other and making her trousers squeak. Or maybe it was her hoof.

I perched on the edge of Brad's desk in front of her, staking my claim to it. *My fiancé. My desk. Got that?*

'What sort of problem?' I asked Brad through a sweet smile.

'I'm being stalked, and I want it to stop,' Aleesha's screechy accent made me wince. Think cockney meets a five-year-old after inhaling a helium balloon and you'll get the picture.

'Do you know who's stalking you?' I asked, wondering why this was a job for Hi-Tec or Brad.

'Well, there's this weirdo who was sending me things a while ago and turning up outside my house and at modelling jobs. I think it's the same guy sending me more stuff now.'

'So why not just tell the police and get them to deal with it?' I asked.

'They did deal with it. Before. This nutter has a

restraining order on him. It went to court and everything. He stopped for a while, but he's started again.'

'If it's happened before, why can't you get him arrested and go back to court?' I shrugged, not wanting to get tied up with this drama queen on what was supposed to be a relaxing pre-wedding week.

'He's denying he's done anything this time.' She ran a hand through her hair and pouted. 'And I can't prove it's him yet. The police said they need evidence he's at it again before they'll do something. I need someone to catch him in the act so I can get him banged up for harassment where he belongs.'

'Aleesha is scared for her safety,' Brad drawled in his Australian twang. 'She wants me to act as a bodyguard until we catch her stalker.'

My head flew round to Brad so fast I thought it might snap off. 'Bodyguard?'

He nodded coolly. 'Aleesha feels that she needs twenty-four hour protection in case he takes things further and tries to attack her.'

Aleesha twirled her hair round a finger and gave Brad a lusty smile.

Yeah, and I bet that's not all she wants.

I suppressed another growl. At least I think I did. A little bit might've slipped out. 'What's your stalker sending you?'

'Chocolate knickers.'

'That's not so bad. I mean, chocolate is a girl's best friend, and you can never have enough pairs of knickers.' Unless you were Aleesha, of course, who obviously had underwear Alzheimer's and frequently forgot to put them on when there were cameras around.

9

'I like going commando myself.' She smirked.

'I hadn't noticed.' I oozed sarcasm.

'Really? It was in *The Sun* and *Celebrity* magazine the last time,' she said proudly. 'I bet Brad remembers, don't you?' She winked at him.

I glanced at Brad, whose face didn't give anything away this time. He wasn't an SAS guy for nothing. Some of the worst people on the planet had interrogated and tortured him, and he never talked. Not that I wanted to know anything about their yucky past relationship. As long as it *was* in the past. I'm sure Aleesha would have no qualms about spilling the beans, though. She was the expert of kiss and tell.

'Anyway, it's sick,' she carried on. 'Who knows what he'll do next. Some celebrities have been killed by their stalkers before, and I don't want it to happen to me. I want him stopped and locked up in the psycho wing before he kills me.' She sat forward and something squeaked again. 'I'm scared,' she whispered, a slight frown of panic forming on her forehead. I say slight, because I don't think the Botox would allow more.

I eyed her suspiciously. OK, maybe I was letting jealousy cloud my judgement of her. Maybe she was a really, really, nice girl. From what I'd heard and seen of her, I seriously doubted it, but no one deserved to be stalked, and what if this guy did go further than sending chocolate knickers?

'Who's the guy that did this before then?' I asked.

'His name's Doctor Spork,' she said.

I burst out laughing. Sorry, couldn't help it. 'Seriously?'

'He changed his name by deed poll. He thinks he's

from planet Spork and says he gets cosmic messages that we're meant to be together.' She sighed. 'He says the Sporkites tell him that I'm really in love with him.'

'Right.' I nodded knowingly. 'I've heard those Sporkites have good taste.'

She did the slight frown again, as if trying to work out if that was a real compliment or not.

'Maybe you'd better start at the beginning,' Brad said to Aleesha.

'About a year ago, Dr Spork started sending me the knickers with these freaky love notes. He'd turn up everywhere when I was doing a modelling job or at my house, with more knickers and stuff. Eventually, the police arrested him, and I went to court to get a restraining order to keep him away from me. The court made him get some psychiatric help and granted the order. He's not allowed anywhere near me.' She ran her tongue over her fake glossy lips. 'After that, I didn't hear anything from him until a week ago, when I started getting the chocolate knickers sent to me again.'

'Were there any love notes with the recent knickers?' I asked.

'No. They were threatening this time. He's obviously realized he can't have me, so now he's threatening to kill me.'

'And has he turned up anywhere near you recently?'

'No. The police have questioned him about it, but he's denying it's him this time.'

'And last time, I take it, he admitted it was him?'

'Oh, yeah. I think he really believed in all that Sporkite stuff.'

I glanced at Brad. 'So maybe it's not Dr Spork this time.'

'That's what I need you to find out.' He stretched out his long, very toned legs and leaned back in the chair.

'Yeah, while Brad's protecting me, you can find out if it is Dr Spork or not.' Aleesha gave Brad a man-eating grin and licked her lips again.

'Haven't you got a boyfriend at home this week to protect you?' I tilted my head.

She waved a hand dismissively. 'Nah. I'm in between men at the moment. Plus, Brad used to be in the SAS. He can probably break someone's neck with his bare hands if he has to.' She eyed his hands longingly, as if imagining those hands all over her. 'He's all the protection I need.'

'Yes, I'm well aware of what his hands can do, thank you very much,' I said.

My stomach flipped uneasily. Brad on twenty-four-hour bodyguard duties with a home-wrecker like Aleesha? I bet her definition of body guarding wasn't the same as mine.

Uh-oh. My perfect life had just turned bad.

Chapter 2

As Aleesha waited in reception for me to have a quick chat with Brad, I shut his office door and leaned against it, giving him one of my best eye rolls.

'You do know what she's like, don't you?' I stared at him, my heart giving a worried little flutter. There was no denying he was gorgeous. Six foot, solid muscle, cropped hair with tiny flecks of grey around the temples, and eyes that hinted at a sense of danger underneath the surface, all gave him that hot, rugged bad-guy look. And it had been a long and rocky journey for us to get back to being together again. I never wanted to risk losing him again. Especially not a week before the wedding.

He came around his desk and pushed his hard body into mine, staring deep into my eyes as he pinned me against the door. 'Are you OK with this?'

'Well, it's a bit late to ask me now. It sounds like you've already made your mind up,' I tried not to sound too huffy, but the scale on my Huff-o-meter was a bit warped and it came out pretty damn huffy.

'You're not jealous, are you, Foxy?'

'Nuh-uh. Not me.'

He tucked a wayward curl behind my ear and then cupped my chin in his hand. 'You know there's nothing to worry about, don't you? This is just a job, that's all. If something does happen to her, Hi-Tec will have to pay out a huge life insurance policy, and what with the recession going on for so long, that's the last thing we can afford right now. This is just proactive insurance.' He pressed himself into me harder. We moulded perfectly together.

He was right. There had been some big insurance claims to pay out lately and Hi-Tec would be struggling if things didn't pick up. The last thing the company needed was another huge loss.

'You're the only woman for me. You always have been,' he whispered in my ear, his breath vibrating against my skin and sending shivers up my spine.

I wanted to believe him, but the green-eyed monster seemed to be messing with my brain. 'So why didn't you ever tell me she was your ex before, then?'

'Because it didn't last long, and she's not important.'

'Uh-huh.' I tried to ignore the tingling sensation as his hand slid round to the back of my neck and stroked that sensitive spot right…oooh, yeah, that's nice.

'You have to trust me.' He carried on stroking.

My insides melted. 'I do trust you.' And I did. After we'd split up and I ended up working for him, he'd done everything in his power to get me back. He'd proved to me that he loved me more than anything, but that didn't mean I wanted to put him slap bang in the middle of possible temptation with someone like Aleesha. 'What about her. I don't trust her at all. And why didn't you tell her I was your fiancé?'

'Because knowing her, if she thinks someone's unavailable, she'll try even harder to get her claws into them. And I'm definitely unavailable.' He leaned forward and brushed his lips on mine. My mouth parted, my tongue seeking his in a fiery show of longing.

Wow. Girly bits hotting up here! Down girl!

I ran my hands up the back of his shirt, pulling him closer.

He leaned back and said, 'Don't worry, Foxy. It's strictly business between Aleesha and me, and I have a sneaking suspicion that Aleesha's probably sending the knickers and notes to herself for publicity. She'll do anything to get in the tabloids. I doubt it's going to take you long to prove it wasn't Dr Spork and it was her all along, so this body guarding thing will be over in a few days.'

I nodded, not wanting to go on about it. I mean, jealousy's not that attractive, is it? I had to trust him. 'So what's the plan?' I asked, wishing I could jump his bones right there and then.

'I'll be accompanying her to modelling jobs, and she's got a daily slot on that TV show called *Real Women* now.'

I laughed. '*Real Women?* Don't you have to have an audition or something to prove you are actually a real woman and not just fake plastic?'

The corners of his lips curled into a grin. 'I'll also be living at her house, too, until this is finished.'

I growled again.

'I thought you weren't jealous.'

'I'm not. Haven't got a jealous bone in my body.' Well, maybe just a teensy one, like my little toe.

'I'll just nip home and get some clothes before I take her back to her house. Meanwhile, you get onto the Dr Spork angle, just in case, then find out if it is

Aleesha doing this to herself for a publicity stunt. Believe me, I don't want to be spending any more time with her than I have to, either.' He slid his arms around my waist, stroking my lower back. 'I can think of much better things to be doing in preparation for the wedding.'

'Oi! What's taking so long?' Aleesha's ugly voice shouted from reception.

I rolled my eyes at Brad again and disentangled myself from his arms.

'There's a file about Dr Spork and the previous court case.' Brad nodded towards his desk. 'Keep me posted, OK?'

I gave him a salute. 'Yes, boss.'

He opened the door and strolled out. From the doorway of his office I watched Aleesha and her camel follow Brad past Tia at reception, and out of Hi-Tec.

I picked up the file from his desk, then went back to mine and flopped down in the chair in front of Hacker.

'Yo,' Hacker said in between tapping on his various keyboards. In Hacker's world, 'Yo' meant 'hello' and 'goodbye'.

I stared at the cake on my desk but, surprisingly, I didn't want it. Usually, bad news gave me an appetite, and I had a sneaky feeling that having Aleesha in my life was definitely bad news. But for some bizarre reason, I couldn't eat it. My appetite had vanished.

Uh-oh. I'd only gone off food once before, and that's when I'd split up with Brad.

Oh, crap. Maybe it was a sign. A premonition that we were going to split up again. I needed to wrap this case up as quickly as possible before I became a statistic on her home-wrecking list, or I lost weight from not eating junk food and my legs became skinny arms like Aleesha's.

Hacker eyed the cake. 'Aren't you eating that?'

I shook my head.

'That's not like you.'

'Tell me about it,' I mumbled.

'Are you ill?'

'Yes. I've got a case of Aleesha-itis.' I jumped to my feet and hurried down the corridor towards the reception desk.

Tia was psychic, although her heebie-jeebie premonitions never seemed to help much in solving cases. But, even if I didn't believe in all that hocus pocus, a girl couldn't take chances. Maybe Tia would have some wacky vision that could help me keep man-eaters at bay.

Tia bent her head over some paperwork, and she didn't hear me approach.

'Pssst,' I said.

Her head shot up, and she smiled. 'Hey, what's up?'

'Are you getting any weird psychic visions about Miss Camel Hoof?'

She frowned. 'Huh?'

'You know, Aleesha the Man-eater.'

'Well…' She tilted her head, thinking. '…no?' It came out more like a question.

I stamped my foot. Childish, I know. 'Nothing?' I pleaded. 'You can't see her running off with Brad and having little baby camels together?'

She bit her lip. 'I can't control when I get the feelings, they just happen. Sorry, Amber, but if I get one, I'll let you know, I promise.'

Growl.

Her huge eyes lit up. 'Ooh, I know! How about we do a spell!'

Yeah, here's the other thing about Tia; she does spells. She makes me do them, too, even though I totally don't believe in them. I just do it to humour her. Really. Usually when she talked me into doing one, something ended up breaking, and I didn't want it to be my heart this time.

I pursed my lips. 'Maybe if I get really desperate, I'll do one.'

'Awesome.' She clapped her hands together and bounced up and down in her chair.

'Right. Better get to work.' I turned on my heels and retraced my steps back to the office to read all about Dr Spork.

I picked up the file and perused through. Dr Spork was born Cecil Oswald Turner-Docherty. Maybe if I'd been born with that name, I'd have changed it, too. He was thirty-one and had no prior police record apart from the original stalking incident a year ago. As Aleesha said, she took him to court and won a restraining order to keep him away from her. The court ordered that he have psychiatric treatment for a delusional disorder and erotomania, whatever that was. It sounded like a good sequel name to *Fifty Shades of Grey*. Since the court case and his treatment, he maintained he'd never stalked Aleesha again. So if it wasn't him, was it Aleesha? She was a publicity hound and didn't care what she did to get in the papers. And if it was him, what had suddenly changed for him to start stalking her again?

I gasped when I saw the name of his court

appointed psychiatrist. Suzy Fox. My sister. Suzy was the serious one in the family, with zilch sense of humour, always perfectly turned out in designer gear. She had very smooth, tidy hair that looked like she'd just stepped out of a Timotei advert. I was the joker with a big mouth, usually found wearing my casual uniform of jeans or combats and Skechers or UGGs. I thought Suzy was cold and detached and she thought I was crazy. Maybe she had a point, but that was probably why we never quite saw eye to eye on most things. If I had to describe her in one word, it would be 'uptight'. I'm pretty sure the last time I saw Suzy crack a smile was in 1980. I'd inherited Mum and Dad's eccentric and quirky genes, but I think hers must've been mutated at birth, or maybe the stork got the orders mixed up, because she was nothing like any of us. Oh, well, maybe having her on the case would make my job easier.

I stuffed the file in my rucksack. 'Yo.' I nodded goodbye to Hacker. 'I have to see a man about a pair of chocolate knickers.'

Dr Spork lived in a small flat in the rough end of town. I parked my car in the communal car park and wondered if it would still have all four wheels when I got back. Jogging up the graffiti-adorned stairway that smelled of cat wee, and probably human wee, too, I emerged on the first floor and pinched my nose. I wandered past the battered and neglected-looking blue doorways along the corridors until I found flat thirty-six and knocked on the door.

A short, squat man with lots of long, dark curly hair opened the door and peered round it. Some of his hair was tied in a skewiff ponytail, threatening to escape its rubber band binding and break free. He was probably the first person I'd met who had scarier hair than I did. He had a bushy beard and, actually, it was hard to tell where his hair ended and his skin began. Still, I bet he was lovely and roasty-toasty in winter, a bit like Sasquatch. He wore jeans with the waistband pulled up high. Any higher, and the jeans would be up to his armpits.

'Are you...Doctor Spork?' I said, stifling the urge to laugh. I know, I'm a very bad girl.

He nodded, glancing up and down the corridor to see if anyone was listening. 'Yes. Is this about Aleesha again?' His eyes widened innocently. 'I've already answered loads of questions from your police colleagues already.'

'Well, I have a few more questions for you, I'm afraid.' I smiled brightly. I wasn't above telling a few white lies to solve a case, and if he thought I was from the police, who was I to put him right? I mean, he thought he was from Planet Spork, and I hadn't corrected him, had I?

He sighed, and his shoulders hunched. 'OK, I suppose you'd better come in.'

His front door opened straight into a tiny open living room-slash-kitchen. It was neat and tidy and in complete contrast to the untidy hair. A giant painting on one of the all-black walls depicted a planet done in purples, blues, yellows, reds, and greens. An old TV sat in the corner of the room with a games console on top, and a two-seater grey checked sofa sat on the opposite side.

I stared at the painting. 'Nice.' It wasn't. It looked a bit like a toddler had thrown up over a canvas after eating lots of M&M's.

He clasped his hands together and smiled with appreciation. 'I did it. It's a painting of Planet Spork. I'm a bit of an artist.'

'I can see. So, where exactly is Planet Spork? I don't think they mentioned it in Astronomy at school.'

'You go past Mars, all the way to Uranus, turn right at Pluto, and it's straight in front of you.'

'Oooookaaaaaay.'

'You don't believe me, do you?' He let out a huge sigh and sank onto the sofa. 'No one does. That's the problem.'

I looked round for somewhere else to sit and spied a plastic chair in the kitchen. 'Do you mind if I get that chair?'

He looked dejectedly at his lap and shook his head. 'No, I don't mind.'

I grabbed the chair and sat in front of him. 'OK, so the stalking thing with Aleesha. What happened?'

'I'm all better now, honestly. The court made me go and see this really good psychiatrist, and I'm all cured. I know now that Aleesha doesn't love me, and she's not really meant to be my wife. I haven't sent her anything lately, like she told the police, honestly.' He gazed up at me with watery eyes.

'So what happened in the beginning, when you were stalking her?'

'Well, I thought the Sporkites from Planet Spork were telling me that Aleesha and I were meant to be together. They told me telepathically that she loved me too, and that all I had to do to win her heart was send her pairs of knickers. The Sporkites are old-fashioned creatures, and they weren't very happy

21

that she kept appearing in the papers with no underwear, you see.' He paused and twiddled his thumbs round and round. 'The chocolate part was my idea, though. I heard that women really love chocolate, but maybe that's where I went wrong. Perhaps Aleesha doesn't really like it that much, and she would've preferred regular cotton knickers.' He peered at me. 'Do you like chocolate?'

Hmm. That was a dilemma. Yes, I loved the stuff, but I didn't think it would be very wise to admit that. I might be next on the knickers list.

I waved a dismissive hand. 'It's gross. Hate the stuff.'

'See, I think that was the problem. Maybe I tried to be too adventurous. I think I should've just sent her some nice, comfortable knickers.'

Yeah, probably nothing to do with the telepathic Sporkites at all.

'Anyway...' I tilted my head in a 'Go on' gesture.

'The Sporkites chose me as their leader.'

'Why?'

'What do you mean, why?'

'Well.' I waved a hand round. 'Why did they pick you instead of, say, Flash Gordon or Captain Kirk? Do you have any qualifications for the job? Just trying to build up a picture here.'

'Er...' He tugged at the end of his ponytail with one hand, thinking. 'Maybe it's because I've got a really big wenis.'

I raised my eyebrows. 'Maybe you shouldn't mention that too often. Nobody likes a bragger.'

He seemed confused for a second, then his eyes lit up with realization. 'No!' He waved his arms around. 'I don't mean that! I mean my *wenis*. Your wenis is the skin on your elbow.' He pinched the skin on his right elbow and stretched it away from the bone, waggling it around.

He was right; it was big. Although I didn't have anything to compare it to. I wasn't in the habit of waggling my wenis.

'The Sporkites have a big wenis, too. Maybe that's why I was the chosen one.'

'Well, you learn something new every day.' I shook my head. 'So, what's the plural of wenis? Wenises or weni?'

He tilted his head and thought for a moment. 'I think it's weenie.'

'That could be it. So, anyway, what else happened with the original stalking?'

'Well, whenever I'd follow Aleesha to her modelling gigs or find out where she was on a night out, I used to think she was sending me secret signals.'

'What kind of signals?'

'When she ran her hand through her hair, it was a signal to me that she wanted me to propose.'

'But you don't think all this anymore?'

He shook his head, and his hair went crazy. 'No. I told you. The psychiatrist told me I was suffering from erotomania and delusions, and now I know that it was all in my head. I'm cured, and I haven't even thought about sending Aleesha any more knickers or notes.'

I pursed my lips, wondering if he really was cured. When I was a police officer for seventeen years, I'd had experience with psychiatrists and people with mental disorders, and half the time you couldn't tell the difference between the doctor and the patient.

23

'Just out of interest, what are Sporkites like?' I asked.

'Well, they're multicolored and small.' He put his hand in the air at a height of about three feet. 'About so high. They have good old-fashioned family values, and they're peaceful creatures. They wouldn't tell me to hurt Aleesha.'

'Right. So, you definitely haven't sent her any more notes or chocolate knickers?'

He put his hand on his heart. 'I swear I haven't.'

'Where did you buy them from before?' I thought it would be a good avenue to check out and see if he was telling the truth. Maybe I could solve this case today by proving he'd bought the knickers, and that would get Aleesha out of my life pronto.

'There's an underwear shop called "Lace" in the mall that sells them. I got them from there.'

My gaze wandered back to the painting. 'Do you still think you come from Planet Spork?'

'Only on a Tuesday.'

'Pardon?'

'There's a time warp that happens every Tuesday, and I can go back and forth between Spork and Earth.'

I did a mental head-banging against the wall. 'Right. So, let me get this straight. You're saying Suzy Fox has cured you of the erotomania thing where you thought Aleesha was in love you, but not of the delusional thing where you think you're Dr Spork from Planet Spork?'

He nodded vigorously. His ponytail fell out of the rubber band and frizzed out like a crash helmet around him. 'I am Dr Spork.'

I stood up to leave. 'Well, thanks very much for

your time.'

He wiped his hands on his jeans and stood up. 'Anytime. It's been nice talking to you. If you fancy a trip to Spork with me, come back on Tuesday.' He smiled.

I closed the door behind me, wondering if he was telling the truth about Aleesha, or whether it was all an act on his part. As an investigator, it was my job to weed out the lies from the truth, and I'd become pretty good at it, if I say so myself. Hundreds of clues give people away when they're telling fibs. Some of them are so subtle—a twitch here, an eye movement here—that they don't even know they're doing it. Unless, of course, they're completely nutso and actually believe their own lies, which could easily be the case here since he was clearly still delusional. But the weird thing was I actually believed him.

Chapter 3

My car still had all four wheels when I got back to it, although I had a rather strange message keyed into the bonnet that said, 'I Went To Sex Shcool'. Charming. I didn't know if they taught any other subjects at sex school, but it was safe to say the pupils would've failed spelling. When it came to cars and hair I was a little accident prone. I'd developed car-wrecking into a fine art, and I didn't really relish the thought of taking the Toyota back to the garage that handled our insurance repairs to get it re-sprayed. The owner already thought I was mad. Can't think why.

As I slid behind the wheel, my mobile rang. I checked the number. 'Hey, Dad.'

'Hi, Amber. What are you up to? Do you want to come round for lunch? Suzy's coming, too.'

Hmm, just the person I wanted to see. Plus, I'd get some of my mum's fab cooking, and since I hadn't eaten my cake this morning, I was probably in dire need of some carbs. Except...I still wasn't hungry, which was totally weird for me.

'I'd love to. See you in ten.' I hung up and motored over to Mum and Dad's house.

I rang the doorbell and Dad, looking incredibly normal for once, answered. He'd been a workaholic policeman for years until his retirement, when he'd swapped workaholicness for depression and didn't know what to do with himself. That was until he started the Neighbourhood Watch Group to rid the local area of dastardly demons. In his mission to fight crime, he'd disguised himself as a tree, a tramp, and an undercover burger chef, amongst other things. It had been a bit of a sore point between him and Mum, since she'd been a police widow when he worked long hours and had hoped to spend more quality time with him after he left the force.

I gave him a kiss on the cheek. 'What, no undercover stakeouts today, then?' I grinned.

He checked over his shoulder to make sure Mum wasn't there. 'Well, you know I've reached an agreement now with your mother where I can do it part time, as long as I don't dress as a tramp again.'

I nodded.

'I was contacted by the security department at the Mall. They heard I caught the thief at Burger Land and wanted to hire me as an undercover store detective, since they've had a spate of thefts going on lately.' He glanced down at his worn jeans and checked shirt. 'I'm just disguised as an ordinary shopper at the moment.'

'I bet Mum's very glad,' I said, remembering the stinky tramp outfit.

'She doesn't know I'm working again yet. She didn't want me to take on anything else leading up to the wedding in case I got too involved, so I told her I've just been shopping for a suit to take to Vegas. Although I think this job could be a way to spend time with her *and* do my Neighbourhood Watch work. You know how she loves to shop!'

'Haven't you got a suit yet?' My eyes widened. 'You've got seven days. No, six days since we're flying out early.'

'Don't worry, I've seen one. I just haven't had time to get it yet.'

'Is that you, Amber?' Mum poked her head out of the kitchen door.

'Don't tell her about the mall job. I don't want her to get the hump with me.' Dad mimed a lip-zipping action to me before I went over to give her a hug.

'How are you?' Mum squeezed me tight.

I could smell the aroma of herbs and spices in her hair. Shame I'd never inherited her cooking genes.

'I'm good, thanks. I'm working on a new case.' I scrunched up my face in annoyance. Usually, I'd be excited at the prospect of solving an investigation, but what with the wedding and Miss Camel Hoof on the block, I felt a bit too twitchy for my liking.

'What case? How can you start a new case seven days before the wedding?' She pulled back, eyebrows furrowed together with concern. 'What about all the last minute things you need to sort out?'

Mum had a way of getting information out of me that I didn't always want to share, and somehow, talking about Brad and Aleesha being in close quarters twenty-four-seven would make me even more stressed. Maybe if I didn't talk about it, nothing would happen. Yep, denial could be good.

I waved a dismissive hand. 'Oh, I'll solve it before the wedding, no problem.' I desperately hoped that was true as I imagined Aleesha trying to give Brad a private full frontal Double FF showing at her love nest.

'Do you want coffee?' Dad asked.

'Ooh, you read my mind. Hey, where's Sabre?' I glanced around for Dad's completely nuts, ex-police

German shepherd dog.

Dad rolled his eyes as we all wandered into the kitchen. 'He's in love.'

'With what?' I dreaded to think. Sabre had a tendency to bang his head, run around like a nutter, and nearly hump people to death. I'd been on the receiving end of a humping-by-sabre incident, and it wasn't pretty. He hadn't been right for a long time, bless him. If he could talk, he'd have some very strange conversations.

'He's in love with a cat.' Mum stirred a pot of chilli on the hob.

'Whose cat?'

'Next door got this rescue cat a week ago, and it keeps coming in our garden for a crap.' Dad pulled a disgusted face. 'I thought Sabre would go mental when he saw it, but it was the weirdest thing. The cat walked up to Sabre like it owned the place, and Sabre went all submissive and flirty.'

I laughed. 'Has he tried to hump it yet?'

Mum shook her head. 'No, not even a mini hump. They spend all their time together snuggled up in the garden now. See for yourself.'

I wandered into the lounge and looked out the doors that led to the garden. Sure enough, giant Sabre lay on the ground looking all Zen-like and calm, which was very unlike him. On top of his back a tiny little black and white kitten kneaded her paws on his fur.

Going back to the kitchen, I said, 'So the diet didn't work to calm him down, but a little kitten did? Strange.'

'Well, if it keeps him calm, I'm all for it.' Dad handed me a steaming mug of coffee, and I set it on the Shaker-style island in the centre of the room.

'Are you hungry?' Mum lifted the lid from a pan of rice and checked it. She waved a hand. 'What am I talking about, of course you are.'

'Actually, I'm not.' I stared at the pans and willed my appetite to come back.

She turned to me and put one hand on her hip. 'OK, what's wrong? Are you and Brad having problems?' She gave me a wide-eyed, worried look. 'Because you know it's perfectly normal to have second thoughts before you get married, don't you?' She pointed a wooden spoon at me. 'But you two are made for each other, so you've got nothing to worry about.'

'Oh, look, Suzy's here.' I pointed out the kitchen window at Suzy's brand new sleek Mercedes pulling up on the drive. If in doubt, deflect the conversation away from yourself.

'Hello.' Suzy walked into the kitchen in a charcoal grey Karen Millen suit and high-heeled stilettos. Her long hair was Timotei advert shiny, and she smelled of exotic flowers.

She rested her Prada bag on the island. I bumped her shoulder against mine, which always wound her up for some reason. 'Hey, sis, how's it going?'

She glanced down at her shoulder like I'd just contaminated her with Ebola. 'I'm very well, thanks for asking.' She perched primly on the edge of a breakfast stool and wiped her shoulder. For a psychiatrist, she had some serious issues of her own.

'I'm glad you're here. I wanted to pick your brain,' I said.

She peered at me, perfectly plucked eyebrows raised in suspicion. Suzy had a tendency of trying to over-analyze Dad and me, which gave me great pleasure in winding her up. I know, I'm a terrible sister.

'Do you finally want to talk about your commitment issues?' she asked. 'Are you calling the wedding off? Because I'm surprised it's gone this far, to be honest.'

'Nope.'

'Have imaginary people been trying to kill you again?' She tilted her head.

'Hey, they weren't imaginary.'

'I see. Not imaginary like the imaginary voices you say you have in your head?'

'No, they're both real. It's just no one has actually tried to kill me again this week.'

She rested her hands in her lap. 'And is that a good thing or a bad thing?'

I chewed on my lip, thinking. 'I can't confirm or deny that.'

'Say the first thing that comes into your head.' She narrowed her eyes.

'Boobs,' I blurted out. God, I had Double FFs on the brain. Damn Aleesha.

She gave me a tight-lipped smile. 'Interesting. And how does that make you feel?'

'What, the word, or the actual boobs?' I asked innocently.

'Either. You tell me; there's no right or wrong answer here.'

'Funny, because I feel like you're going to give me a detention if I don't say what you're expecting.'

'With you, nothing would surprise me.' She took a napkin off the island, unflapped it, and put it neatly on her lap.

'Anyway, I want your professional opinion on something,' I said as Mum dished up bowls of chilli and rice and set them in front of us.

'Are you joking? You're always making light of my work.' Suzy studied the bowl carefully before picking up a fork and eating the tiniest morsel, chewing about three hundred times before she swallowed.

Mum and Dad, used to our banter, tucked into the food happily and ignored us.

'You've got a patient called Dr Spork.' I forced myself to pick up the spoon and take a bite, but I wasn't remotely interested in it. At this rate, I'd turn into a skeleton before the wedding, and I didn't fancy being a dead bride.

Dad nearly choked on his chilli from laughing. Mum glanced up and giggled.

'I know, that's what I thought,' I said to them.

'Are you mocking the mentally ill?' Suzy glanced at us all with horror.

'No, I don't discriminate,' I said. 'I mock all sorts of people.'

'That's the trouble with you.' Suzy poked her fork in my direction. 'You can never be serious.'

'And your trouble is you're *too* serious. Life's too short to be serious.' And anyway, I could be serious when I wanted to be. I was seriously getting stressy thinking about Aleesha trying it on with Brad.

Suzy let out a big huff. 'I can't talk about a patient, anyway, it's confidential.'

'Not even to your sister? I swear it won't go any further.'

She huffed again. 'Why do you want to know about Cecil, anyway?'

I put the spoon to my mouth again but couldn't take a bite, so I set it back down and stared at the chilli as if it was a bowl of mouldy sprouts. Leaning my elbows on the island, I told her about Aleesha, the stalking, and the chocolate knickers fetish.

'I've seen her in the paper,' Mum said. 'She's that trashy slut who's always showing off her arse.'

'And more,' Dad said, then glanced up at Mum's raised eyebrow. 'Not that I've looked.'

'How could you not look? It's in your face in all the papers. And she's always having affairs with married men and trying to break up relationships.' Mum's nose wrinkled up with distaste.

See, it wasn't just me that thought Aleesha was a lady-garden-flashing home-wrecker! Maybe I was right to be worried, after all.

'Dr Spork's been improving very well under his treatment regime.' Suzy dabbed at the corners of her mouth delicately with the napkin. 'I don't think he would do anything like that anymore.'

'I bet they said that about Hannibal Lecter, and look what happened? He escaped and ate lots more people,' I said.

'That was a film!' Suzy scoffed.

I shrugged. 'So, it could happen.'

More huffing by Suzy. 'I can only tell you what's already a matter of public record, and you seem to know all that anyway. Dr Spork was diagnosed with a delusional disorder and erotomania.'

'So, what is erotomania, exactly?' I asked.

'It's basically a form of delusion, where the person believes someone, usually a higher person or celebrity, is in love with them. Sometimes erotomanics believe the person they're fixated on is sending them secret signals to show their love.'

'So, when I was about seven and I had a crush on Bagpuss, was that erotomania?' I asked, slightly worried.

Suzy pinched her lips. 'You had a crush on Bagpuss?'

'Oh, yes,' Mum piped up. 'Don't you remember when Amber went through a stage of thinking she was a cat? She'd wear this ridiculous headband with pointy ears on the top and crawl around the house, purring. And she was totally obsessed with Bagpuss.'

Suzy peered at me, eyes narrowed.

Uh-oh, here we go. I knew that look. Suzy was about to analyze me. She reached into her bag and pulled out a notebook and pen. She quickly scribbled something down and then glanced up at me as if waiting for me to go on.

I decided I'd better not mention that I asked advice from my cat, Marmalade. Suzy would probably have me sectioned. Even though Marmalade did usually give good advice.

Suzy's eyes narrowed further, her pen poised above her pad, ready to take more notes. 'So, you had a crush on a big, pink cat?'

'Yes, I think we've just established that.' I secretly thought that the only thing psychiatrists did all day was repeat what people said back to them, just so they'd know how stupid it sounded. I already knew it sounded stupid, but in my defence, I was a kid. Didn't you ever have a secret crush on something, or pretend you were an animal when you were little? No? Er...OK, moving swiftly on, then.

'Do you want to talk about your crush on

Bagpuss?' Suzy asked with excitement, feeling the whiff of a perspective patient. 'You could have underlying disorders from it. It could be the reason you have commitment issues now.'

I gave her a 'Get real' look. 'I don't have commitment issues.'

'Oh, really?' She scribbled something down furiously on her pad. 'You could've fooled me. I've had to listen to so much drama about your on-off relationship with Brad for God knows how long. First you wouldn't commit to Romeo, and now you've had a hard time setting the date for your wedding to Brad.'

'Well, it's been complicated! I didn't commit to Romeo because, even though I loved him, it wasn't enough. I think subconsciously I knew I was always supposed to be with Brad. And, anyway, Brad left me straight after he proposed and disappeared for months. That would give anyone commitment issues!'

'Yes, but honey, he was on an SAS job.' Mum patted my hand. 'He couldn't tell you where he was.'

I knew that now, but at the time he just upped and vanished with no word. What was I supposed to think? I was out of my mind with worry. I didn't know whether he'd left me for someone else or he'd been killed. I'd gone through a living hell, imagining all the possible scenarios, and sunk into a dark depression. Apparently, it would've compromised his mission to contact me, but by the time he'd come back, I was so hurt and devastated that I couldn't even speak to him, let alone see him. He'd left a scar on my heart that had taken a long time to heal. My whole world had crumbled without him in it, and I tried to block him out of my life for a long time. I tried to forget my feelings for him because I couldn't go there again. I couldn't put myself through the nightmare of not knowing whether I'd ever see him again. And it had worked, for a while. At least that's what I convinced myself of. I'd started seeing Romeo. We were partners on the Special Operations Team at Hertfordshire Police for a long time before we became partners in the bedroom. He was a great guy, and he got me over the Brad saga. I'd loved Romeo, too, just not in the same way I loved Brad. Then when I got kicked off the police force, Brad had wasted no time in offering me a job with Hi-Tec, and he'd wasted no time in trying to get me back, either. I'd resisted for a long time, but the walls around my heart couldn't keep Brad out forever. So, yeah, maybe I did have commitment issues, and maybe there was always that fear in the back of my mind that he'd leave me again. But going through bad times made you realize just how precarious life was. It brought home just how much you had to lose the second time around if it didn't work out. Not that I would ever tell Suzy, though. She'd jump all over it and hound me forever to talk through my feelings.

'Anyway, you don't have to worry about him leaving you again now he's given up the SAS,' Mum said, as if reading my mind. She knew me too well.

Suzy made more notes on her pad. 'And have you seen Romeo lately? Does he know you're marrying Brad?'

'Our paths have crossed during some investigations. I haven't said anything to him about the wedding, but I'm sure he would've heard it from some of my old friends at the police.' I paused, desperately hoping Romeo was happy. I'd never meant to hurt him. It's just that love was a complicated thing, and the rules sometimes got blurred around the edges.

'You're not eating.' Mum nodded to my food. 'Are you sure you're OK?' Then her eyes turned the size of dinner plates. 'There's something you're not telling me, isn't there? You *have* split up with Brad.' Her hands flew to her cheeks. 'That's the only time you've ever lost your appetite in your life.'

'Not yet, I haven't!' I blurted out. That was the trouble with me, sometimes my mouth acted before my brain.

Mum's hand flew to her chest. 'Oh, no! Has Aleesha got her sights on your man? That little slut!' Before I could answer, she carried on, 'Right. This is serious. You're supposed to be getting married in seven days! I've got my hat and my outfit! The Vegas tickets are booked!' Her voice rose to screechy parrot level.

Suzy looked smugly at me. 'I knew something was wrong. Go on, tell me what Brad and Aleesha are up to together.'

I threw my hands in the air. 'Nothing's wrong! I've just got…indigestion, that's all,' I fibbed. God, I'd never get out of here. How did this conversation get to be about me all of a sudden? 'Yes, I admit that I don't want Aleesha anywhere near Brad, but I trust him completely. Nothing's going to happen.' I hoped. 'I just want to get her out of my life as soon as possible so I can get back to being excited about the wedding, which is why I need some help on this case.' I glared at Suzy. 'Let's stop talking about me and talk about Dr Spork.'

Looking disappointed, Suzy put the pad and pen on the island.

'Can erotomanics get out of control? Become dangerous? Or is it just a harmless crush?' I asked.

'There is usually an obsessive element to the delusion. And eorotomanics have been known to stalk their victims. Sometimes they will go to extremes to get what they want.'

'How extreme?'

'Well, sometimes they send the person love letters or flowers and chocolates, that kind of thing. They sometimes make phone calls or turn up wherever the other person is.'

'What about threatening letters? Would they send threats to kill the person?'

'It's possible, if the erotomania is getting out of control and they feel rejected.'

So, had Dr Spork progressed from sending love notes to sending the threatening ones? 'What sort of treatment have you been giving him?'

'A mixture of drugs and cognitive behavioural therapy.'

'And you think it's working?' I seriously doubted it, if he went to Planet Spork on Tuesdays.

'I'm confident his erotomania is now cured, although it can reoccur. He knows perfectly well now that Aleesha doesn't secretly love or want him, and she isn't sending him telepathic signals via the Sporkites.' She frowned. 'So, in my *professional* opinion, I don't think he would be responsible for sending Aleesha any more chocolate knickers or letters.' She emphasized the word 'professional' and looked at us all like we were a bunch of idiots.

'OK, how about the delusional thingybob? He still

thinks he's from Planet Spork.'

Her lips tightened. 'We're still working on the delusional disorder, but I'm confident it won't be long before I've cured him of that, too. I don't see how I can be of any more help. I don't think he's the one stalking her now.'

'Dad, Dr Spork said he bought those chocolate knickers at Lace in the Mall. Can you stake out the shop while you're working and see if he buys them?' I asked.

'What do you mean, working?' Mum asked Dad.

Oops.

Dad sighed. 'I was going to tell you.'

Mum folded her arms across her chest. 'Tell me what, exactly? You haven't got another Neighbourhood Watch thing going on, have you? I thought you were spending lots of time at the mall looking for a suit.'

Dad shot me a look before turning to Mum. 'They needed someone to help them catch shoplifters. What was I supposed to do? I haven't been working all day like before, have I?'

I rummaged in my rucksack for the office file and pulled out a photo of Dr Spork, thrusting it at Dad before Mum could have a go at him. Since they'd reached their agreement of Dad only going undercover part time, they'd been enjoying a second honeymoon period, and I didn't want to upset the apple cart. 'Here, this is him.'

Luckily, that distracted her. 'He looks quite normal,' Mum said, peering over Dad's shoulder as he examined it.

'For Sasquatch,' I said. 'Anyway, Jeffrey Dahmer looked normal.'

'Yes, but didn't he torture animals before he started killing people?' Dad said. 'I mean, that's a dead giveaway for a potential serial killer.'

'That's not *always* the case,' Suzy said.

'Has Dr Spork tortured any animals?' I asked Suzy.

'Not that I know of. He believes Sporkites are peaceful creatures, and they wouldn't telepathically tell him to do any harm to someone.'

I didn't point out that believing in Sporkites in the first place had to be a dead giveaway for something, too.

'OK, Dad, if you can keep a look out for him at the Mall, plus anyone else buying chocolate knickers, I'd really appreciate it.'

'Yep. I'll get down there straight after lunch.'

'Ooh, I know! I'll come, too,' Mum said. 'I always wanted to look in that shop. I heard they had some really nice French maid's outfits.'

I pulled a face. Definitely too much information. Maybe the second honeymoon period for them was really working.

Chapter 4

I rang Brad on his mobile with the hands-free as I drove away from Mum and Dad's with the windows open for some fresh air.

'Speak,' Brad said when he picked up.

Brad didn't have very many traits that annoyed me, but the way he answered the phone was one of them. I did some heavy breathing down the phone.

'Are you running, Foxy?'

'Me? Exercise? Are you joking?'

'Well, stop doing heavy breathing, then.'

'Stop answering the phone like that, then. Anyway, are you and Aleesha at her house? I want to ask her some questions.'

'Yes.'

'How's the body guarding going?'

'I'm not really doing much at the moment. Aleesha's flouncing around in a flimsy dressing gown and reading magazines.'

My eyes became slits. 'It's three o'clock. Why's she in a dressing gown?' She was dressed earlier, even if she looked like a cheap hooker. No offence to hookers.

I pulled up at a traffic light next to an old man in a classic convertible, roof down.

'Because *Celebrity* magazine is coming here later to do another article, and they wanted shots of her showing off her assets in some sexy underwear.'

'You mean her boobs?' The word 'boobs' came out a lot louder than I anticipated.

The old man in the convertible looked over at me and gave me a nod. 'Yes, please!'

Oh, God, what was happening to me? I was getting mammary Tourettes now. Aleesha was so bad for my health.

Brad lowered his voice. 'Don't worry. I'm staying well away from her.'

'How can you stay away when you're guarding her body?' I sped away from Mr Leery Convertible.

'Look, she does nothing for me. You're the only woman I want.'

I went all gooey and melty inside. 'Really?'

'Really.'

'Really, really?' And now I was turning into a lovesick teenager. Argh!

Jealousy and neediness are not attractive, Amber. Get a grip!

'Anyway, I have a chaperone,' Brad said.

'Who? Another poor man she's got her hooks into?'

'Her twin brother. He's her PA and accompanies her on all her jobs.'

I brightened up then. Surely, nothing would happen if her brother were there. 'Right, I'll be there soon.' I attempted to act like an adult again.

Ten minutes and no more boob outbursts later, I arrived at Aleesha's six-million-pound mansion. Acres of Hertfordshire fields surrounded a ten-foot wall around the property, and tall iron gates enclosed it at the front with an intercom system. A couple of cars were parked on the road outside, paparazzi guys with big cameras, probably hoping to get another crotch shot before dinner. Ew. That was enough to put me off my dinner, if I wasn't already.

I pressed the intercom.

'Yes?' A muffled voice filled the air.

'I'm Amber Fox to see Aleesha, please.'

'I'm buzzing you in now,' the voice said.

I drove through the pristine gardens, counting no less than six water features, and towards the main house. It looked more like a palace or stately home. How had she got this much money just from flashing off her boobs? Maybe I was in the wrong job. The only thing un-palace-like was the stonework. Originally a nice golden-beige colour, or even white, it was now painted turquoise. Yes, you heard me right. It was a turquoise monstrosity, with turrets and towers and imposing chimneys.

The colour made my eyes go funny as I pulled to a stop on the stone driveway and stared at it. I never wanted to see the colour turquoise again. It would haunt me forever.

I rang the bell, also turquoise, and looked at the step, which was, yep, you guessed it, the T-word again.

A man with short bleached blond hair and black eyebrows answered the door. He was skinny, with lots of blingy diamond studs in both ears. He wore black leather trousers that looked like Aleesha's, and a tight black satin T-shirt. I think he had makeup on, too. Eyeliner, mascara, a bit of blusher and...I peered closer...pink lip-gloss, if I wasn't mistaken. I guessed this was the brother. I also guessed he wasn't exactly straight.

'Hi!' he gushed, tilting his head. 'You must be Amber!' His voice was high-pitched like an excited school kid. 'I'm Nathan, Aleesha's brother, but you can call me "Nate". Come in.' He sashayed inside, beckoning me to follow him. 'We're all in the kitchen, getting cosy.'

Grrr. Hopefully, not too cosy.

With the age of the old manor-style house, I expected antiques and lots of original features, but the whole place looked like it had been stripped of anything from the original era and replaced with modern décor. The walls, turquoise. Ceiling and cornicing, white (thankfully). Doors, pink. Seriously? Yak. And it got worse. Furniture, grey and black. Kitchen worktops and appliances, red.

I pinched the bridge of my nose, feeling a colour headache coming on.

Aleesha sat at a black polished table in the centre of the kitchen, wearing lacy red underwear under a sheer turquoise cover up. Although I think she should've sued the manufacturer under the Trade Descriptions Act, because it didn't actually cover anything up. Still, at least she had underwear on for a change. She sat next to Brad, giggling about something and leaning conspiratorially towards him.

Brad gave me a look as if to say, 'Help'. Aleesha ignored me.

'Here we all are!' Nathan sing-songed and sat down next to Brad, angling towards him, too, with a look of adoration.

'So, anyway, that's when I had a wardrobe malfunction, and my nipple fell out on live TV!' Aleesha touched Brad on the arm, the charms on her bracelet jangling together, and threw her head back, laughing.

I fought the urge to vomit.

'Ahem.' I coughed.

'Oh, hey. I didn't see you there.' Aleesha glanced up at me. 'So, what have you found out?'

'Not much so far.' I sat down opposite Brad and felt his foot touch mine. At least I hoped it was his. I glanced up at him, and his eyes widened a fraction, as if he was telepathically telling me to get him out of there.

'Well, that's not much use then, is it?' Aleesha glared at me.

'I need to ask you some more questions.' I tried to avoid touching the table surface. Who knew what she did on it.

'OK, so shoot, I haven't got all day. I'm being photographed soon.' She turned away from Brad, who looked relieved, crossed her legs, and tapped her fake nails on the table.

'I spoke to Dr Spork, who denies he's been sending you the knickers and letters. I also spoke to his psychiatrist, and she believes he's got over his obsession with you.'

She shrugged. 'Well, they would say that, wouldn't they?'

'Maybe. Maybe not. Have you had any other stalkers over the years?'

'Yeah, 'course I have. In my job, it's pretty normal. Men just can't get enough of me.' She flashed me a smile. Probably fake teeth, too.

'Oh, everyone loves Aleesha.' Nathan clasped his hands together. 'The men can't get enough of her. Some women, too.' He nodded proudly.

'Have these other stalkers ever sent you things as well?'

'Oh, yeah. I've had vibrators, offers for weekends

away, expensive underwear, love songs, letters. Some rich guy even wanted to buy me an island in the Caribbean!' She sounded pretty pleased with herself.

'And you didn't take a hint when you got the expensive underwear?'

'Huh?'

'Never mind.' I shrugged. 'So, it's not exactly unusual for fans to send you things?'

'Nah.'

Which made my job harder. It could be anyone sending stuff to her, or it could indeed be a publicity stunt by Aleesha herself. 'What's so unusual about these knickers, then, that you think you're in danger and need a bodyguard?' I glanced at Brad.

'Well, it's the letters with them. The horrible threats.' She did one of those tiny Botox frowns again.

'Show her,' Nathan said.

Aleesha got up from the table and swaggered out of the room, making sure Brad got an eyeful of ass. When she returned, she had a few sheets of paper in her hand, a brown Jiffy envelope, and a pair of chocolate knickers. Thrusting them in my direction, she said, 'Here, these are photocopies of most of the notes. The police took the originals, along with the knickers, but since they can't find out where they're coming from and there were no fingerprints on them, they're not doing anything to help. Which is why I hired Brad.' She squeezed his shoulder.

'Amber's the best investigator there is.' Brad flashed me a proud smile. 'I'm sure she'll find out who's responsible very quickly.'

Did I detect a hint of pleading in his voice to solve

the case and get him away from her?

'That last Jiffy envelope came this morning with another pair of knickers and a letter inside.' Nathan nodded at the pile.

I read the letters:

'Die, you bitch. Die.'

'I will get you back.'

'I'm going to kill you.'

'You should be ashamed of yourself.'

'Slut.'

'I'll kill you if it's the last thing on earth!'

OK, so the slut one was pretty normal.

'Can I take this last one?' I asked.

Aleesha nodded warily at it like the letter was about to spring to life and paper-cut her jugular.

If it was Aleesha or Nathan sending them for publicity, she was doing a good job of looking scared for her life. In fact, the terrified look she sported now was the only thing about her that didn't seem fake. Maybe Brad's hunch that it was Aleesha wasn't right, which meant I would have to investigate every angle.

I stuffed the letters in my rucksack. 'When Dr Spork sent you the knickers before, what did his notes say?'

'They weren't like these ones. They just used to say how much he loved me and how we were supposed to be together and stuff. He bombarded me with them every time I showed up somewhere at a job or club, or he'd hang around outside the house and either throw them at the car or leave them outside the gate. One time he managed to get inside the grounds and left me a pair by the swimming pool outside. They melted.'

I mulled that over in my head. I supposed it could be a copycat stalker, trying to pin the blame on Dr Spork. Probably plenty of people in the crowds would've seen him giving her the knickers before. Plus, the media coverage about the case had been huge, thanks to Aleesha giving another crotch flash as she arrived at court to get the restraining order. It could be someone who was obsessed with her, or someone who hated her. Sounded like there were a lot of those about.

'Creepy, huh?' Nathan pulled a lemon-sucking face.

'I don't want to turn into John Lennon,' Aleesha shrieked.

'I don't think there's any chance of that,' I said.

'No, I mean, usually stalker's behaviour escalates, doesn't it?' Aleesha glared at me. 'They try harder and harder to get the attention of the person they're harassing until it gets out of hand.'

'Well, the stalker is obviously trying to get your attention about putting some knickers on for a change. I'm sure he's not the only one that would appreciate not seeing everything on full display,' I whispered under my breath.

Aleesha narrowed her eyes at me, and her lips pinched into a thin line.

Oops. From that little look, I'd have to say I didn't whisper it as quietly as I thought.

'I don't want to get killed by the stalker,' Aleesha snapped. 'He doesn't seem to be giving up, and I don't expect he's suddenly going to just change his mind and stop threatening me.'

Nathan nodded vigorously. 'You have to help us.' His mascaraed eyes pleaded with me.

I studied the Jiffy envelope and postmark. 'Do they all usually arrive like this?'

'Yes. All in the same kind of envelope. All with a local postmark by regular post,' Nathan said. 'I do all Aleesha's secretarial stuff and PA work, so I always check the mail.' Nathan batted his eyelids at Brad, maybe in the hope he wanted any dicktation or other secretarial work doing.

I pulled out a pen from my rucksack to pick up the knickers and examine them. I hoped they were unused, but you never knew. They had black nylon and elastic on the edges like regular knickers, with weird edible chocolate in the middle. I didn't even want to think what the chocolate part was made of. If the chocolate melted, or got eaten or licked off (ew!) you'd be left with just a pair of black crotchless knickers.

'Are these exactly the same kind as the ones Dr Spork sent you?' Brad asked Aleesha.

'Yeah. Exactly the same.'

'Have you ever had any other death threats?' I asked.

'No.'

'Really?' I found that hard to believe. I bet a few jilted ex-wives in the background dreamed up ways to get her back after their men had had affairs with her.

'Everyone loves Aleesha.' Nathan smiled adoringly at her. 'Who could be doing this?'

'I don't know, but believe me, I'm going to find out. And quick.' I stared at Brad, who gave a slight nod of his head. 'What about your collection of ex-husbands or fiancés? Did any of them hold a grudge?' I leaned forward. 'How many have you

49

had, out of interest?'

'I don't know. I lost count after fifteen.'

I think I snorted then.

'There was Jon, the footballer,' she started. 'I mean, he was a bit pissed off I divorced him for Tyrone, the backing dancer, but that was ages ago. Then Chris, the pop star, was a bit angry when we split up. He trashed me in the press.' She pulled a 'can-you-believe-it' face. Aleesha obviously didn't like the taste of her own medicine.

'Then there was Curtis, who came to do some plumbing work for me.' She grinned at us.

'Yes, what about him?' I asked.

'Well, he released a sex video of us together. It went viral.' She looked pleased about that.

Brad swallowed, probably hoping there wasn't one of him with her out there somewhere.

'I sued him, but he didn't have much money, so I didn't get much in damages out of him. He wasn't too happy about it, though.'

'What about Stig?' Nathan piped up. 'He went a bit nuts when he caught you in bed with his brother.'

'Stig?' Brad asked.

'He's in that rock band, The Hell Devils,' Aleesha said. 'Yeah, I think he was a bit pissed off.'

I sighed. 'OK, I'm losing count now. Who out of your exes was angry with you lately or made any kinds of threats?'

'Probably just Stig and Curtis.'

'Anyone else you can think of who might want to threaten you?' I asked.

'Don't think so. Oh, wait.' Her finger shot in the air. 'I had a bit of an incident with my cleaner a month ago and had to sack her.'

'What sort of incident?' Brad asked.

'Well, she was nicking stuff from me and selling it on eBay. I caught her red-handed with my mobile phone, the bitch. She was going to sell my text messages to the tabloids, then sell the phone. I kind of hit her.'

'How do you "kind of hit" someone?' I asked.

'OK, I did hit her. She reported me to the police, and I got arrested.' She wobbled her head like a petulant child. 'I mean, come on, I was the victim, and they arrested me!' She paused, and then a smirk lit up her face. 'Still, I made sure it got on the front pages, and she got done for theft. Win-win all round, I'd say.'

'What's the cleaner's name?' Brad asked.

'Tracy White.'

'How about any rivals in the glamour world?' I asked.

She flicked her long hair over her shoulder. 'No. They're not a patch on me.' She tapped a fake nail to her head. 'See, I've got the business sense and the PR sense. They just use their bodies. I mean, there are plenty who must be jealous of me.' She flashed her teeth in a smug smile. 'But I haven't had any threats from other glamour models.'

'What about the TV show you've just started?' I asked. 'Do you have any rivals on the set of *Real Women*?'

'Well, there was a bit of trouble with Jessie Hinds, who used to be on the show.' Aleesha stared at her nails.

'What sort of trouble?' Brad asked.

'The show is basically two women chatting about lady things and interviewing guests,' Nathan said.

'Typical daytime TV stuff. The presenters were the comedian, Tania Tate, along with Jessie, but then Jessie got thrown off the show because she was useless, and she blamed our Aleesha for replacing her.' Nathan threw a dramatic hand in the air. 'I mean, can you believe it? Jessie thought she could just turn up and put in a below average performance because she was screwing the producer.'

My brain whirred away at that little snippet of info. I remembered seeing the show a few times in the past. Jessie had a lively personality and was pretty funny. Hmm. Jessie was sleeping with the producer. Jessie gets kicked off the show. Then Aleesha gets put on the show. Had Aleesha been screwing the producer to take her place? I wouldn't put it past her.

I eyed her. 'How did you get on the show? You haven't done TV work before, have you?'

'I'm branching out.' She tapped the side of her head with her nails. 'See, I've got the brains to diversify. Increase my audience. I know what my public wants, and I'm going to give it to them.'

'Yes, but did they approach you or did you approach them?'

'Well, I might've known the producer.'

'In what way? In a "sleeping with Jessie's boyfriend" kind of way?' I asked.

She shrugged. 'What can I say? I'm attractive to men! I can't help it if they all want me.' She winked at Brad and flipped her hair over her shoulder with a hint of arrogance.

A growl lurked in my throat.

'Come to think of it, I think the producer, Steve, might've been a bit pissed off with me, too.'

52

'Really?' I drawled. 'And why would that be?'

'Well, I kind of dumped him for Alfonso, the racing car driver, after he gave me my slot on the show.'

I couldn't keep up, and I was quickly losing the will to live. 'Is that everyone you can think of that might be holding a grudge against you?' I prayed it was.

She shrugged. 'I think so.'

I stood up to leave and looked at Brad. 'Can I have a word with you, *boss,* before I go?' I jerked my head towards the kitchen door.

Brad nodded and followed me along the hallway, out to my car.

'How did you ever get involved with that?' I asked.

'I keep asking myself the same question. We were both a bit drunk and—'

I held a palm up in the air. 'No, don't tell me any gory details. Otherwise, I'll be picturing you with her, and that's just gross.' I did a mock shiver. 'This is a nightmare. It could be anyone stalking her. Lots of people hate her, and probably with good reason.' I glared at him. 'I'm supposed to be having a nice chilling-out week before we jet off to Vegas to get married. I should be spending my time getting my bits and bobs waxed into the shape of a heart; now I'm stuck trying to find out who wants to threaten that trollop.'

Brad rested a hand on my arm. 'I'll make it up to you on the honeymoon, I promise.' His voice turned husky, his eyes crinkling at the corners as he smiled.

I poked him in the chest. 'You'd better.'

I needed to speak to Jessie. Maybe she'd been so

angry with Aleesha for not only stealing her boyfriend but also stealing her TV spot, that she'd resorted to death threats. Then again, maybe Steve felt like Aleesha used him to get on his show and wanted to teach her a lesson. Or it could be any one of her harem of exes. Or another woman she'd pissed off by sleeping with her man. It could just as easily be one of the gazillion people in the world who just hated her. Stars attracted attention, and she always seemed to attract the wrong kind.

The possibility of solving this case before the wedding was getting less and less likely. And what if I didn't find the stalker in time? Would Aleesha be accompanying us to Vegas so Brad could guard her body and keep her safe? Over my dead body!

Chapter 5

As I sat in my car in front of the turquoise eyesore, I phoned Hacker, font of all data held on a computer system in the whole universe.

'Yo,' he said. 'How's it going?'

'Don't ask. Have you got a pen? I've got a lot of people I want you to look into.'

'Fire away.'

'Chocolate knickers.'

'Haven't tried wearing them before, do they chafe?'

I chuckled. 'I want you to check the following people's online purchases to see if they've ever bought any. Jessie Hinds, Steve Palmer, Stig from The Hell Devils, Chris Mayfield, Curtis Jones, and Tracy White.' I explained who they all were.

'Not a problem.'

'Do the usual background checks on them, while you're at it. And let me have their contact details, too. I'll need to speak to them all.'

'Whose details do you want first?'

I glanced up at the sky. They probably all had a reason to hate her. It was a case of 'Eeny meeny miny mo'. I plucked some names out of the air. 'Jessie Hinds and Steve Palmer.'

'OK, I'll call you back in a minute. Yo'

I hung up and sped down the driveway as fast as I could. Since everyone neglected to offer me a drink back there, I needed coffee. I pulled up outside Starbucks, which was like my second home, and jumped out of the car. Standing in line, I stared at the muffins, cinnamon pastries, and brownies, willing myself to want one. Usually, I'd be lusting after them, but today, I couldn't even muster up even a flicker of excitement.

'Hey, Amber,' Becky, the young barista, said to me. Since I was such a regular, we were now on first name basis. 'Do you want your usual? A large mochaccino and lots of cakes?'

'Hi, Becky. Nope, just make it a mochaccino, please.'

She frowned slightly. 'Are you feeling OK?'

'Upset stomach,' I offered. Just because I knew all about her ex who'd cheated on her, her university exam results, and her latest tattoo, didn't mean I wanted to share my life details, too.

'OK, coming up.'

I waited at the end of the counter until my coffee was ready and took it out to the car just as Hacker rang.

'Yo. What've you got for me?' I asked.

He rattled off some addresses and phone numbers for Jessie and Steve, and I jotted them down in my notepad. 'I'm still looking into online purchases for the knickers.' Then he lowered his voice. 'I Googled them, and they actually look pretty cool. Do you think Tia would like some?'

'No! They're tacky and...sticky. And the chocolate doesn't even look like real chocolate. Anyway, I'm sick of hearing about people's sex lives today.' What with Mum and Dad, and finding out about Brad and Rampant Camel Hoof, I never wanted sex again. In fact, I was going to be a nun from now on. Well...after I married Brad, then maybe after the honeymoon, and...OK, maybe I wouldn't be a nun. I think I'd sworn too much in church to be accepted, anyway. That had to be a big no-no on the application form.

'All right,' Hacker said. 'I'll get onto to the other stuff and let you know.'

'Cool. Yo.' I hung up and dialled Steve, who was working on a TV show at the Elstree Studios. He said he'd give me security clearance to get in, and I drove the forty minutes with an annoying woman on the Satnav providing directions.

Pulling up to the studio gates, I wound down my window and smiled at the security guard. He looked suspiciously like Tom Baker, one of the actors who played *Doctor Who* when I was growing up. I remembered watching the daleks and cybermen from behind a pillow, and I especially liked Tom Baker because he came to our town once for a *Doctor Who* Fest when I was a kid. He gave me a jelly baby in the shape of a bus, which was so cool. I dropped it in the dirt, though, but he gave me another one. Bless him.

'Hello,' he said in a booming, friendly voice. 'Can I help?'

I peered at him. 'You're not Tom Baker, are you?'

He chuckled. 'No. I get mistaken for him all the time.'

I wasn't convinced. If he really were Tom Baker, it would be a bit of a let-down going from *Doctor Who* to security guard.

'Do you like jelly baby buses?' I asked, thinking I could catch him out.

He pursed his lips. 'Can't say I've ever seen one.' But his eyes twinkled as he said it.

Oh, yeah, he was so Tom Baker.

'I'm Amber Fox to see Steve Palmer.'

Tom/Guard glanced down at a clipboard and nodded. He handed me a pass with 'Visitor' stamped on it and gave me directions to the right studio.

I clipped the pass on and found a parking spot between an old Jag and an Aston Martin that looked like it should be in a Bond movie. I made my way to reception, where a young blonde woman at the desk gave me a perky smile.

'Hi, and what can I do for you today?' She practically bounced up and down in her chair.

'I'm looking for Steve Palmer. I'm Amber Fox, we have an appointment.'

'Oh, yes, he told me you were coming in.' She pointed to a set of doors to her right. 'Go through the double doors, past three offices on the left, the kitchen on your right, and he's in the first studio you come to. You'll see *Real Women* on the door, but they're not filming at the moment, they're just setting up for tomorrow.'

'Thanks.' I smiled and made my way to the studio. This was so cool. I'd always wanted to be on a TV set. When I was a kid, I went through a stage of wanting to be an actress. That was before I wanted to be an astronaut or Wonder Woman.

I wandered past an empty kitchen area with a microwave, kettle, fridge, and hob on one side and some chairs and tables on the other, and came to a set of large double doors. I tentatively opened them and stepped inside. People were setting up cameras, lights, electrical wires, and other funny-looking equipment that looked like hairy squirrels. There was a raised stage set up at one end with a panel of chairs for the presenters and interviewees on the show.

One of the men fiddling with a camera glanced up at me. 'Can I help you?'

'I'm looking for Steve.'

He pointed to a tall guy with buck teeth, ginger hair, and an abundance of freckles. 'That's him.'

Steve wasn't the kind of good-looking guy I'd imagined as Aleesha's type. Then again, anyone probably would've been her type if he could give her career some publicity.

As I approached, Steve was deep in conversation with a petite girl, no more than about nineteen, with mousey hair and thick glasses.

'Yes, Steve,' the girl said, nodding her head at him so hard her glasses slipped down her nose. 'Anything else, I can do for you? Anything at all?'

'No, that's it, Felicia, thanks.' He turned to me as Felicia gave him an adoring look and scurried off.

Hello. Someone had an ickle crush on Stevie Boy.

'You must be Amber Fox.' Steve held his hand out.

I shook his sweaty hand and cringed inside, wondering how many germs got passed around shaking hands throughout the world in one day. It didn't bear thinking about.

'Nice to meet you.' I let go of his hand and wiped it surreptitiously on my jeans.

'You mentioned on the phone it was about Aleesha being threatened?' He led me to the corner of the studio where we could talk in private.

'Yes.' I explained about the knickers and the

threatening notes.

'Well, it wasn't me. What has she told you?' He frowned.

'She mentioned that maybe you weren't happy she split up with you after you got her a slot on the *Real Women* show.'

He sighed and shook his head angrily. 'She's a conniving cow. I thought she really liked me.' He paused for a beat. 'Look, we had a bit of a…fling. She's one of these people that, even though she's loud and trashy, people love to watch. A bit like rubber-neckers at a car wreck. She convinced me, in…' His face turned red as he fumbled for the words to use. '…in a moment of passion, that she could get the ratings on the show higher. They'd been slipping for a while, and *Real Women* was in danger of being axed. So I took Jessie off the show and put Aleesha on. The ratings have never been higher. The public love watching her trash the guests, and she seems to get on well with Tania Tate, the other host. There's a good spark between them.'

'Right. And so after you got Aleesha on the show, she dumped you for someone else, is that right?'

'Yes. But I've got no hard feelings.'

'And what about Jessie? Did she have any hard feelings? I mean, you two were an item, weren't you? As well as her being a presenter on the show?'

His face took on a redder shade. 'Look, I'm not proud of having a moment of weakness and having a…fling…with Aleesha. I never meant for Jessie to find out, and I never meant to hurt her.' He leaned in closer. 'I was engaged to Jessie before this happened, and I want her back, but she's not interested.'

60

'Really? I can't think why. I mean, you slept with someone else and got her fired. Not exactly a good start to an engagement, is it?'

His eyes widened, and he looked like he'd just been caught with his pants down in the library. 'Jessie won't speak to me now, and I really love her still,' he mumbled. 'I never should've succumbed to a moment of weakness with Aleesha, but, I swear, I've never threatened her. Why would I threaten to kill her? I need her on the show now. If she's not here, the ratings will go back down, the show will be cancelled, and I'll lose the producer's slot.'

I studied him carefully. He didn't seem angry, just embarrassed about the whole thing. Plus, he was right. What did have to gain by threatening her? He needed her on his side.

'Well, thanks for your time.' I spotted Felicia standing to our side, pretending to be watching what the camera operator was doing but more likely eavesdropping on our conversation.

'You're welcome.' Steve gave me a relieved smile.

I wound my way round the equipment, heading for Felicia, and saw the comedian and co-presenter, Tania Tate, come into the studio. She had a weekly sitcom series running every Friday night about a French family who'd taken over an English bed and breakfast, kind of like *'Allo 'Allo* meets *Fawlty Towers*. She was in her late thirties, short, with black spiral curls down to her shoulder blades. Maybe one of them would have a useful tidbit of information for me.

'I got all the way home and realized I'd forgotten my reading glasses!' Tania rolled her eyes at Felicia. 'I'd lose my brain if it wasn't attached.'

'I saw them here somewhere earlier.' Felicia glanced around the studio, frowning. 'Now, where were they?' She wandered off to search for them and I sidled up to Tania.

'Hi, I'm Amber Fox.' I smiled at her and reached out a hand to shake hers. 'I'm a big fan.'

Tania grinned. 'Thanks. Nice to meet you.' She pumped my hand enthusiastically.

'I'm looking into some threats Aleesha's received and wondered if you had any ideas about who could be doing it.'

'Aleesha's getting threatened?' Tania raised her eyebrows in shock. 'Well, I know she has a bit of a reputation for being difficult, but I actually get along really well with her. We seem to have a good vibe together on the show, and I like her down-to-earth attitude.' She leaned in conspiratorially. 'Much better than all this up-your-own-arse pomposity that a lot of the TV people have. All the fame seems to go to their heads, you know? At least Aleesha is staying true to her roots and just being herself.'

Well, that was one way to look at it, I supposed.

'So you didn't hear anyone on set threaten Aleesha?'

'No. And I really don't know her well enough to have a clue who might be doing it. What sort of threats are they?'

'Death threats.'

'Wow. Pretty serious then? But, then, I think probably most people in the public eye have received some sort of threats or unwanted public attention in their career. It's probably nothing to worry about. Just some crackpot who's a bit bored.'

Maybe, maybe not. 'Well, if you think of anything

that might be helpful, can you let me know, please?'
I handed her my card.

'Of course.' She smiled at me as Felicia came bounding over like an excited puppy.

Felicia handed Tania a beige glasses case. 'Here they are. They were in the kitchen.'

'Thanks very much. What would I do without you?' Tania left us both with a smile.

Felicia pushed the glasses up her nose, even though they hadn't fallen down. *A nervous tick, methinks.*

'I know who you are. I heard you introducing yourself,' Felicia said softly.

'And you're Felicia?'

'Yes. Felicia Seabright.'

'What do you do here, Felicia?'

'I'm taking media studies at university, and I'm doing an internship here.' She gave me a pinched smile. 'I help out on set three days a week.'

'Do you have much to do with Aleesha when she's here for the *Real Women* show?'

She tutted angrily. 'That hussy! The woman is so rude to people. And so needy. She flounces around like she owns the whole world, and she treats me like a piece of dirt. Someone needs to teach her some good old-fashioned values, like wearing more clothes, and some manners.'

Interesting. And would Felicia be the one who wanted to teach her some? 'You don't like her much, do you?'

'No.' She narrowed her eyes, which looked kind of scary since they were magnified about a squillion times behind the thick lenses. 'She's a floozy, a tart, a trollop, and a heathen.'

I agreed with the first bits, but a heathen? What did that have to do with anything?

'Aleesha's been getting threatening letters and other things.' I didn't mention the knickers. Maybe I could catch her out if she was the one sending them.

'Well, it's not me!' Her mouth formed into a shocked *O*, and her glasses shot down the end of her nose. She pushed them back on with a finger. 'I don't like the...' She puckered up her face, as if trying to think of a suitable word. '...floozy, but I wouldn't threaten her.' She chewed on her bottom lip for a second. 'I did hear Jessie threaten her before she got thrown off the show, though.'

'What happened?'

Felicia's gaze darted around, and she lowered her voice. 'Well, when Jessie found out that Aleesha had replaced her, they had a blazing row in the studio. Jessie said she'd kill her.'

I raised an eyebrow, thinking if Aleesha had just slept with my fiancé and lost me my job, I might threaten to kill her, too. But had Jessie actually acted on that and sent the letters and knickers? I mean, we all make threats in the height of anger that we would never actually carry out.

'When was this?'

'Two weeks ago.'

And the letters started a week ago. Maybe Jessie had been stewing away with anger for a week before she decided on a campaign of threats to get her revenge.

'OK,' I said, giving her a beaming smile. 'Thanks for your help.'

I left her standing there frantically adjusting her glasses. I wasn't convinced about Felicia yet. Maybe the freaky eyes made me disbelieve her, or the fact that she seemed nervous. Maybe it was because Aleesha treated her like crap. Or maybe because she obviously had a thing for Steve Pants-Down, and jealousy and unrequited love did funny things to people. Still, if Jessie had threatened Aleesha, I had to take it seriously.

Chapter 6

It had been a long day. Right about now, I should've been craving junk food and a sugar rush. But as I drove back to the now empty barn conversion I shared with Brad, instead of a rumbling in my stomach, I had what felt like angry birds there, pecking at my insides. Tonight I had to sleep in our big bed alone, and God knows what the sleeping arrangements would be at Aleesha's house.

On the way home, I called Hacker and asked him to check out whether Felicia Seabright was a secret chocolate knickers-buyer online.

As I opened my door, Marmalade, my ginger cat, greeted me. He sat there giving me a look as if to say, 'What time do you call this? I was hungry hours ago.'

I scooped him up in my arms and rubbed my chin against his head. 'God, you're heavy. I think you need to go on a diet.' Since I'd moved in with Brad, Marmalade had been doing starving kitty eyes at both of us, playing one off against the other to see how much food he could get. Brad obviously thought the way to a woman's heart was through her pussy, so he was obliging in the 'spoil Marmalade' stakes. Looked like Marmalade's little ploy was working, the sneaky devil.

Marmalade purred in response as I carried him into the kitchen and poured half the usual amount of gross-smelling kitty biscuits into his bowl. He stared at the bowl, then looked up at me in disgust at the miniature portions.

'Hey, if you don't want it, I'll take it back!' I wagged a finger at him.

That got him going. He practically jumped in the bowl before I could whip it away and started tucking in.

OK, I talk to my cat. That's not so weird. I often ask him questions, too, and I'm convinced he's some kind of magical cat who understands English. What? That doesn't make me mad. I like to think it makes me more sensitive and in tune with wildlife. Well, that's my story, and I'm sticking to it.

I opened the fridge door and peeked inside. Usually, Brad did the cooking. I couldn't cook anything without burning it or giving us food poisoning. I still wasn't hungry, but I needed to eat something before I wasted away. I pulled out a bowl of lasagne that Brad had made the night before, removed the tin foil covering, and set it on the granite breakfast bar with a spoon.

Wine. What I needed to unwind was lots and lots of wine. I turned round and rummaged in the wine cupboard, pulling out various bottles of red. French or Chilean? I wiggled the bottles, trying to decide. I uncorked the Chilean, grabbed a glass out of the dishwasher, and poured a hefty-sized drink. I was just gulping it down and feeling a lovely, mellow relaxation in my clenched stomach muscles when I heard a noise behind me.

Marmalade had his head stuck in the lasagne and was busy scoffing it.

'Hey!' I put the glass down and picked him off the

breakfast bar. 'You little piggy.'

I sat him back on the floor, and I swear he gave me a 'what-do-you-expect-when-you don't-feed-me-much' shrug.

The lasagne was ruined now, so I scraped the remains into his bowl. He purred loudly in appreciation before wolfing it down. I told you he was sneaky.

I picked up the glass of wine and gulped some more. 'Do you think Aleesha's going to try it on with Brad?' I asked Marmalade. 'Meow once for "yes" and twice for "no".'

Marmalade looked up, seeming to think about the question for second. 'Meow.'

Grr. 'That's exactly what I was thinking.' I was reaching for the bottle again when Hacker phoned.

'Yo,' I said wearily.

'Yo. You OK?'

'Mmm.' I swallowed more wine. 'I'm getting drunk. I'll be better when I've finished the bottle.'

'You worried about Brad being with Aleesha?'

'No!' I gave him my best shocked voice.

'You don't have to worry about him. He loves you more than anything. He can't wait to marry you, you know.'

'Uh-huh.' I knew that. Deep down, I really did. But then, didn't Steve say he loved Jessie, too, and he cheated on her. The thing was, you could never really be sure, could you? It wasn't like you could crawl inside someone's head and examine their thoughts. Anyway, I didn't want to think about it anymore; it would fry my brain and turn me mad. Well, madder than I already was.

'Tia told me to ask whether you want to do a spell

with her to solve the case and get Aleesha out of your life for good.'

Tempting. 'Hold that thought. I might have to resort to that in a few days if I haven't got anywhere. Have you found anything out?'

'None of the people you mentioned bought any of the knickers online, but I guess they could've got a friend or relative to do it for them. They're sold on hundreds of websites all over the world, and someone could just go and buy them from a shop with cash, so, it's probably a dead end.'

I pouted to myself. Damn.

'Curtis Jones, the plumber, declared himself bankrupt after Aleesha sued him about the sex video, so he might still be a tad pissed off with her. I looked into Tracy White, and she's now got a criminal record for stealing Aleesha's phone. She hasn't worked since the incident, and I think it would be pretty hard to get a job as a cleaner if your clients know you've got sticky fingers.'

'Very true. What else?'

'Jessie hasn't managed to get another TV show since she got fired from *Real Women*, so she's probably not too happy, either. Stig's been out of the country on a tour with The Hell Devils for the last six months, so he can probably be crossed off the list. And Chris is now happily engaged to an American model and living in the States, so I think it's highly unlikely he's still interested enough in Aleesha to send her threatening mail.'

'What about Felicia? Did you find anything out about her?'

'Not much. She lives with her parents, her Dad's a vicar, she's in her final year at university, and she hasn't bought any knickers online or anything else that might be interesting.'

So, that explained the heathen comment. Felicia could be a happy-clappy religious fantatic, which might be a motive. Aleesha had to be breaking a hell of a lot of moral laws. 'Thanks.' I finished the last mouthful of my wine and poured more.

'Do you want some company? I could come round with Tia.'

'No, you two love birds have a good night. I'll just drink another bottle.'

'OK, if you're sure. Yo.'

'Yo.' I hung up and dialled Brad.

'Speak.'

'In a land, far, far away, there was once a beautiful princess called Amber. She was about to marry her handsome prince, when all of a sudden, a plastic serving wench rode into town on a donkey covered with fleas and—'

'Foxy, have you been drinking?'

I stared at the almost empty wine bottle. 'Yes. I'm doing a good job at polishing off the wine store.'

'I miss you.' His voice turned husky.

My heart did an excited loop-the-loop. 'Me, too. It's really quiet here without you.'

In the background, Aleesha screeched, 'Braaaaaaaad! Where are you? Nathan's made you nettle tea, and I've got strawberry jam for you.'

I pulled the phone away from my ear and glared at it before putting it back. I could understand the tea, since Brad always drank the herbal crap that smelled like boiled up beetles. But the jam? What was she planning on doing with *that*?

'She's driving me mad,' he said.

'You and me both. What's the jam for?' I felt myself inflating with anger, Hulk style.

'I dread to think.'

'Well, you must know,' I said accusingly. 'Why jam? You don't even eat it?'

'I don't know, honestly. She's definitely not getting near me with it, Foxy. Trust me.' His voice softened.

He was right. This was just a job for him. That was all. And what kind of marriage wasn't based on trust? I deflated and told him about Steve and Felicia, and what Hacker came up with so far.

'So, no further forward, then,' he sighed.

'It could be anybody.'

'I still think she's doing it herself. You need to get me out of here,' he whispered into the phone. 'If it's not Aleesha trying to jump on me, I've got Nathan, too.'

'So, what are the sleeping arrangements over there tonight?'

'I'm in one of the many guest rooms, and I'm locking the door and barricading it with some heavy artillery.'

I chuckled at that. 'Well, I'll be here in our big old bed, playing with my pussy.' I glanced at Marmalade.

He let out a growl then, but it was a lusty one, not a jealous one. 'I'm imagining it already.'

'Braaaaaaaaaaaaaaad,' Aleesha called out. 'Where are youuuuuuuuuu? The jam's going cold.'

I rolled my eyes. 'You'd better go. I can't stand that screeching.'

I pictured him rolling his eyes, too, as he said, 'Me, neither. Night, Foxy.'

'Night, Braaaaaaaaaaaaaad,' I said, mimicking Aleesha's voice.

I'd just hung up when Dad phoned. It was like British Telecom Central tonight.

'Hi, Dad.' I scooped up Marmalade and set him on my knee, stroking him behind the ear.

'Hi. No news to report from Lace. Your mum and I staked it out all day and didn't see Dr Spork or anyone else buying chocolate knickers. Mum bought six pairs herself, though, to take to Vegas with us.'

Omigod. It sounded like they were having a better sex life than Brad and me at the moment. Even Sabre was getting more action in the romance department than I was, and that was just beyond bizarre!

'Thanks for sharing that.' I scrunched up my face.

Marmalade burped. His sensitive feline ears probably didn't want to hear about Mum and Dad's bedroom activities, either.

'I'll go back tomorrow as soon as they open and see what happens.'

'OK, thanks, Dad. Goodnight.'

I took Marmalade and the rest of the wine to bed and passed out around midnight, but I couldn't sleep properly. The bed felt cold. As I tossed and turned until the early hours, all I could think about was Aleesha creeping into Brad's bed in the middle of the night, smearing jam all over him and licking it off.

Chapter 7

I was up bright and early the next day. No, scratch that. I wasn't feeling bright; I was feeling grumpy again. My appetite was still in limbo, so I downed two strong hazelnut coffees, thinking that at least I'd get some protein from the hazelnuts. It was still too early to see Jessie, or Curtis, the amateur porn video star, so after feeding Marmalade, I headed to the office.

Hacker was already there when I arrived, clacking away on his keyboard, as usual. Today his hoodie said 'Illest'. Was that even a word? And what did it mean? Maybe the person who went to sex shcool could tell me.

'Yo.' I dumped my rucksack on my desk and flopped onto the chair.

'Yo, you look like crap.'

'Thanks.'

He grinned. 'So, how's the case going?'

'It's going nowhere fast.' I frowned. 'Have you managed to dig anything else up for me?'

'Nothing that will probably help.'

I swivelled in the chair, thinking. It squeaked loudly as my swivelling got faster. 'I'm pretty sure Steve isn't involved. Jessie has a good motive and threatened to kill Aleesha. Tracy and Curtis may have had good reasons to threaten her, but I won't know more until I talk to them. Felicia could be a

73

runner, too. Or any other members of the public who hate Aleesha. If I can't catch someone out actually buying the knickers, then I'll have to stake out the suspects we have to see if they take a little trip to the post office.'

'And how are you going to follow all of them at once?'

I sighed. Usually, Brad would help me with stuff like that, but he was tied up with Camel Hoof. Not literally, I hoped. 'I'll have to get Dad to help. And I bet Tia would. She's always itching to get involved in investigating.'

'Ooh, can I? Can I? Can I? That would be totally awesome!' Tia suddenly appeared in the doorway carrying a bag of doughnuts and two cups of coffee. Today she wore yellow leggings, furry red boots, a fluffy yellow jumper, and red lipstick. She looked like Big Bird. How could she tail someone wearing that lot?

Bouncing up and down with excitement, she spilled some coffee out of one of the cups. 'Oopsie. Better clear that up.' She dumped the doughnuts and coffee on my desk and disappeared to find a cloth to clean up the brown stain on the carpet.

'Bless her,' I said. 'If she thinks a stakeout is going to be exciting, you're obviously not spicing up her life enough.' I raised an eyebrow at Hacker.

My mobile rang as Tia reappeared to clean up the mess. 'Morning, Foxy,' Brad's sexy Australian accent sounded down the phone.

'Morning. How was your night? I hope Aleesha didn't try and play tents with you while you were smeared in jam.'

He chuckled. 'I've had better nights.'

I sat forward in the chair. What did that mean? Better what? 'Better nights in general or better sex?'

'How could you even think I'd have sex with her? I'm a one-woman guy, and that woman is you.'

Was I being unfair, thinking something might happen between them? Probably, but would you trust Aleesha with your man? Nope, didn't think so. I mean, I know it takes two to tango, and all that, but Aleesha practically served sex on a plate.

'How was your night?' Brad asked.

'Boring. Hopefully, I'll solve the case today, and we can get rid of Aleesha.' Wishful thinking. And I definitely had something in mind to do with that jam.

'I hope so. If she says "Braaaaaaaaaaaaaaaaaaaaaad" in a whiney voice one more time, I'm changing my name.'

'Yeah, good luck with that.'

'Another letter and pair of knickers arrived this morning in the post.' Brad's tone turned serious.

'What did it say?'

'It said, "You won't be alive much longer, bitch, so enjoy it while you can."'

'Catchy. Maybe Hallmark will use it.'

'Foxy?'

'Yeah.'

'I love you, and I can't wait until Vegas. Six days to go.'

I smiled, and my stomach did a gooey little 'ahhhhhhhhh'. 'Me, too.' Six days, and I still needed to get the undies, manicure, and bikini wax. I hung up and stared at the phone with a goofy grin plastered all over my face.

'Er...Amber, there's someone in reception to see

you,' Tia said from the doorway. 'He said his name's Dr Spork.'

I sniggered. I couldn't help myself. Maybe he'd come to confess. I seriously hoped so.

He looked like he'd had a bit of a spruce up from yesterday. His hair was semi-tidy, tied back in a ponytail with a red scrunchie. He held a package, wrapped up in pink paper with a pink bow on top. He wouldn't meet my eyes as I stood in front of him.

'Dr Spork. How are you today?' I eyed the package suspiciously.

He shrugged. 'I'm OK, thanks.' He thrust the package at me and ran out the door before I could say anything else.

I glanced over at Tia, who raised her eyebrows in a big question.

Uh-oh. I had a horrible feeling. Whenever anyone sent me packages, it was never good. I'd had human noses, foxes' heads, spiders, and all sorts. I could take a guess what was in this one. For once, why couldn't someone send me something nice? Was that too much to ask?

I tore off the pink paper. Inside was a cardboard packet that contained a pair of chocolate knickers and a note.

I groaned, unfolding the note as Tia stood over my shoulder and read with me:

'I love you, Amber, and I know you love me, too. The Sporkites told me last night in a dream that we'll be together soon, but in the meantime, please wear the chocolate knickers so you'll be thinking of me.

All my love
Dr Spork xx'

Icky, icky, ick. My skin crawled, and I fought the urge to scratch myself. It looked like Suzy's therapy wasn't working after all. Still, one thing was certain. I know people can disguise their writing, and Hacker had some handwriting analysis software on one of his computers that would confirm it, but I was pretty sure by looking at the love note that it wasn't the same handwriting as the threatening letters Aleesha had been getting. So the good news was I'd soon be able to eliminate him as a suspect, hopefully. The bad news was that I was now the subject of his erotomania.

'Ew,' Tia said. 'That's gross.' She pulled the knickers out of the box and examined them. 'That's not even real chocolate, is it?'

'I dread to think what it is.'

'Ooh, talking of chocolate, did you have one of the choccie doughnuts I left on your desk? They're super fab.'

'No.'

'No?' she practically shrieked in my ear. 'Quick, go and get one before you pass out from lack of sugar.' She peered at me. 'I think you're losing weight, and you won't be able to fit in the dress Dad made.'

Tia's dad was the famous fashion designer, Umberto Fandango, whose life I'd saved once. He'd designed my amazing wedding dress and fitted it to perfection for me.

'OK, I'll have a sniff of one.' I left her with the knickers.

'What do you want me to do with these?' She hurried after me and waved the knickers under my nose.

Hacker looked up from his desk, eyes lit up as he stared at Tia and the knickers. 'I can think of something.' He gave her a sexy grin.

She stopped waving them and grinned saucily back.

I looked between both of them as they gave each other 'let's-try-them-out-later' looks.

'Get a room!' I rolled my eyes.

Tia let out an embarrassed cough. 'Right. Well, I'll just get rid of these then, shall I?' She disappeared back to the reception desk. I heard her unzip her handbag and zip it up again.

Handing Hacker the love note from Dr Spork and the threatening letter Aleesha had given me, I said, 'I'm pretty sure the same person didn't write these, but I need you to compare them with your super-duper software.'

'Sure thing. I'll let you know.'

I downed the now cold coffee that Tia had brought, sniffed a doughnut as promised, and grabbed my rucksack, heading out the door before anyone sent me anything else.

I dialled Suzy on the hands-free as I drove to Jessie's house. 'Hey, sis, how's things?'

'And to what do I owe the pleasure of an early morning phone call?'

Why was I surrounded by people who couldn't answer the phone like normal people? A simple 'Hello, how are you?' would be nice.

'A big, cheery good morning to you, too,' I said. 'I'm very well, thanks for asking. How are you on this fine and chirpy morning?'

I think I heard a 'Hmmph' on the other end, followed by, 'What do you want? I'm very busy.'

'I think you need to get Dr Spork back in your office quick. He's sending me love notes and knickers now.'

She gasped. 'Not possible. He's cured of the erotomania.'

'Oh, no he isn't.'

'Oh, yes, he is.'

Before this quickly turned into a pantomime script, I said, 'You told me yourself it could reoccur. Hypnotize him, or give him some electric shock treatment, or a lobotomy, or...I don't know, something, whatever it is you do.'

I got a bigger gasp that time. 'Electric shock treatment? Lobotomy? We're not living in the Dark Ages, you know. Psychiatry has come a long way from electric shock treatment and lobotomies.'

'Well, maybe you should start using them again. I got an electric shock off the toaster once, and I couldn't remember anything for a couple of seconds. Imagine if you gave him a full blast. You could knock the erotomania right out of him.'

She sighed. 'I'll see what I can do.'

'Well, whatever you do, do it fast.'

She hung up on me then, and I stuck my tongue out, even though she couldn't see me. The young girl in the car next to me could, though. She stuck hers out in return and gave me a two-finger salute. I dreaded to think how many road rage incidents had been caused by mistake.

I pulled up outside Jessie's detached house in the nearby village of Sawbridgeworth at nine a.m. Posh and Becks used to own Beckingham Palace there. Jessie's house was nowhere near as big and grand, but it must've set her back a hefty amount. Before she got her slot on *Real Women*, Jessie had been in the popular soap *The Village*. She'd started on the show as a child actress and grown up in front of the viewers' eyes, until they killed her off in a spectacular car accident. Apparently, it was Jessie's decision to leave *The Village* to try moving into film work, but after her one and only film role flopped, she'd moved onto daytime TV. Jessie always seemed to have a lot of fans, though, so I was surprised she'd been axed from *Real Women.* I hoped, for her sake, she had some other work lined up.

My feet crunched on the gravel driveway as I made my way to her heavy wooden front door. Ringing the bell, I glanced around. Bushes hid the overgrown garden from prying eyes on the street. The curtains were closed. The porch light had been left on all night and had attracted a ton of moths. I stepped back a notch, not wanting to get one of those buggers in my hair. I'd probably never find it again in all the curls, and it might lay eggs.

I waited a few minutes before ringing the bell again. The curtain twitched at a front window. Half of Jessie's face came into view before disappearing behind the curtain again.

'Go away!' she yelled from inside. 'I don't want to sign anymore autographs.'

I bent down, opened the letterbox, and said, 'I'm not an autograph hunter. My name's Amber Fox, and I'm investigating some threats Aleesha's been receiving.'

'That bitch? She deserves them. Go away!'

'No, I really need to talk to you.' I'd stay there all

day if I had to. I had a case to solve and a wedding to look forward to. Plus, I still needed my lady bits waxing. 'I'm staying here until you answer my questions.'

'Are you from the police?'

'No, I'm an investigator with Hi-Tec Insurance.'

'What's insurance got to do with Aleesha?'

'She's got life insurance with us.' I whispered, 'unfortunately,' under my breath. 'If anything happens to her, we'll have to pay out a claim, so I'm investigating the threats.'

She yanked the door open suddenly. The last time I'd seen her on TV, she was perfectly made up, with her choppy black bob all glossy and neat. Today her skin was blotchy, and her hair was more scarecrow than sleek. She wore a dressing gown that looked like she'd lived in it for a week.

'Have you got any ID?' She narrowed her eyes with suspicion.

I pulled out my staff ID and handed it over for her to peruse.

Satisfied, she thrust it back in my direction. 'Well, hurry up, then. I haven't got all day.' She stood back to let me in and slammed the door shut.

'Thanks. Have you got another show to get to?' I tucked my ID into my pocket and followed her down the cream hallway, into a large conservatory at the back of the house.

'No. Not thanks to Aleesha.' She sat in a rattan two-seater sofa, tucking her legs underneath her and picking at a bitten fingernail with chipped nail varnish.

I sat opposite. 'I heard about what happened with you getting fired from *Real Women.*'

She went into picking overdrive but didn't look up. 'Yes. God, that woman is so conniving. She set out to get Steve and my job. I hate her. We were engaged, you know, but she thinks any man is fair game. You should see her.' She threw a hurt gaze my way. 'She comes over all nice and seductive until she's got her claws into a guy and got what she wants from him. She doesn't care who she hurts in the process.' Jessie sniffed. 'And I haven't had any other offers for work since my film flopped. That's the trouble with show business. Everyone's so fickle.'

I pushed the thought of Brad and Aleesha together out of my head again. Was Aleesha trying to get her fake nails into Brad at this very moment, like she did with Steve?

'I'm sorry. It must've been very upsetting for you.'

'Of course. It still is. I loved Steve, and I loved doing *Real Women*. I was really good at my job, too. ' She threw a hand in the air in a hopeless gesture before it plopped onto her knee, and she resumed picking.

I knew how she felt, too. A while ago, my archenemy Detective Inspector Janice Skipper had connived to get me thrown off the police force. She'd gone to extraordinary lengths to block all my chances of promotion, make up lies about me, and take credit for investigations that I'd solved. And all because she was jealous of my relationship (at the time) with Romeo and was after him herself. She tried every sneaky little thing she could to split us up. Maybe that's why I was so wary of Aleesha's obvious interest in Brad. I'd been there before. If Aleesha was anything like Janice Skipper, and I suspected she was, I knew she'd stop at nothing to get what she wanted and wreck people's lives in the process. Oh, yes, I knew all about vicious women and had a great deal of sympathy for Jessie.

'Were you upset enough to threaten to kill her?' I asked.

She glanced up sharply. 'What's that cow said to you?'

'Actually, it wasn't Aleesha that told me you threatened her at the studio. Apparently, a lot of people heard it.' I wondered why Aleesha hadn't told me that little snippet of information herself, but then she hadn't really been that forthcoming. Maybe she was embarrassed about what she'd done. Nah. I instantly dismissed that idea. Silly me. Aleesha didn't seem embarrassed about any of her actions.

Jessie's lips pursed together. 'Yes, I admit I threatened to kill her, which wasn't very professional of me. But after what happened with her and Steve, I couldn't believe she was getting my slot on the show, too. I was furious and upset when I found out, which is why I flew off the handle. I bet loads of people threaten to kill people every day and never act on it. It's just a figure of speech.' Her sad brown eyes met mine.

That was true. I'd threatened to kill Suzy numerous times when we were growing up, especially that time when she stole my *Doctor Who* collection of plastic daleks and pulled their exterminating guns off. I'd spent months saving up my pocket money to buy them and they were ruined in a couple of minutes.

'Why would I want to waste my time and energy threatening Aleesha? I don't want anything to do with her ever again. And anyway, I'm not going to let it ruin my life. I'll get some more TV work eventually, and I'll get a better man, too. One who won't cheat on me.' She looked up into my eyes, her chin raised with determination.

'So, you haven't been sending her letters or any packages of knickers?'

'What? No! Of course I haven't.'

I believed she was telling the truth. Even though she was an actress, the shock on her face seemed 100% genuine to me. It must've been tough to be a child star, with all that expectation and pressure in the dog-eat-dog world of show business, but there was still a hint of innocence in her eyes. Although Jessie was upset, as I would be, she seemed like a strong character who would bounce back from this. And somehow, I couldn't really see her lowering herself to send Aleesha threatening letters.

'You know, if it's any consolation, Steve wants you back.'

'Well, he can go fuck himself!' She picked a piece of skin from around her fingernail and drew blood.

OK, maybe not that innocent.

'I wouldn't touch him now after he's been with that tart. You don't know what she's got.'

'If he's prepared to cheat on you, you don't deserve him anyway.'

'Thanks.'

I stood up and smiled. 'Well, good luck with the job hunting. I hope you find something.'

Another possible suspect had just bit the dust.

84

Chapter 8

Next stop, Curtis Jones. I knew the address since Curtis now lived on the same run-down housing estate as Dr Spork. Oh, what joy. Either I'd get another word-slinging genius defacing the car again, or I might get chocolate-knickered to death. I couldn't decide which was worse.

I parked the car and glanced around for any yobs. A scruffy stray cat with a ripped ear and dirty face looked a bit mean and vicious, but since it was highly unlikely he could claw graffiti into the metal, I thought it would be safe. Curtis lived on the fourth floor, so I hoped Dr Spork wouldn't be out and about and spot me. Plus, it was Tuesday. With any luck, he was on an intergalactic journey to Planet Spork.

I climbed the stairs to the fourth floor and banged on Curtis's door.

It swung open, and a beefy guy in his early thirties with a bald head and tattooed sleeves on his arms said, 'Are you from the council about the damp problem, because I can't believe you've housed me in this place?'

My first thought was that Aleesha had very wide-ranging taste in men. Pretty much anything that had a pulse or...other bits. From rock stars to pop singers, racing car drivers, and plumbers, Aleesha didn't discriminate. Maybe she'd win the Equal

Opportunities Award one day. My second thought was that I wondered whether he actually polished his head, which was so shiny it looked he'd overdone it with the Mr Muscle and a duster.

'Sorry, no, I'm not from the council.' I tried not to stare at the sunlight reflecting off his head. 'I'm Amber Fox. I need to ask you a few questions about some threats that Aleesha's been getting.'

He narrowed his eyes at me. 'I never want to hear that manipulating bitch's name again.' He leaned on the doorframe and folded his arms. 'If it wasn't for her, I wouldn't be living in this bloody place. She's ruined me. I used to have a lovely house in a nice part of town, and now I'm stuck in a damp bed sit.'

'She's been getting threats to kill her.'

'So?'

'Have you been sending her threatening letters?'

'No.'

'How about knickers?'

'No.'

'Your name has come up as someone who might have a grudge against Aleesha.'

He raised a disinterested eyebrow. 'Oh?'

'Can you give me any answers that contain more than two letters and don't have an O in them? We'll probably be here all day otherwise.'

He thought about that for a moment, chewing on his bottom lip. 'What do you want to know? I don't want to talk about her any longer than I have to. Even her name brings me out in hives.' He pulled the neck of his T-shirt down and pointed to his skin. 'Have I got hives forming?'

'Not yet.'

'OK, you'd better make it quick, then. When they

come up, they're so itchy I'm scratching for days.'

'Can you tell me about your relationship with her and what happened when she sued you over the sex video?'

He sighed. 'Well, she called me out to look at a blocked drain, and I've had nothing but shit off her since! Actually, it was her brother, Nathan, who arranged the job. So I went over to her place and sorted out the blockage in the downstairs toilet, and she was, you know, prancing around the house pretty much naked and flirting with me.'

A few red dots appeared on his neck, but I didn't tell him. 'Then what?'

'Well, we had a bit of a thing.'

'A thing?'

'OK, we had sex. Everywhere. In the Jacuzzi, in the bedrooms, in the kitchen, in the—'

I held up my hand. 'OK, OK, I get the gist.'

'Then she says she wants to film it, so I thought why not? It's a bit of a turn on, you know. So we went into her bedroom, and she had this video camera set up at the end of her bed, all ready, like. And we had some more sex.'

'Right. So after the sex part?' I gestured for him to hurry up, trying not to imagine them together.

'Well, she gave me the video and said it would make a nice souvenir for me. Then she pretty much hinted that I should put it on the Internet.'

'Hinted how? What exactly did she say?'

He stared up at the sky above my head, thinking. 'Well, I can't remember exactly, but she said something like, "Wouldn't it be a shame if this got leaked?" Then she winked at me, paid me for the plumbing work with a hefty tip, and pretty much

87

chucked me out of the house.'

'So, you made the video public?'

'Yeah, why not? It was what she wanted, and I didn't care. The camera was pointing so you couldn't see my face, just hers. But it was a setup, because then she bloody sued me for every penny I had. Said I caused her emotional distress and damage to her reputation.'

I snorted.

'Yeah, exactly. I lost my house to pay the legal bills, and I had to give her all my savings for damages. I was left declaring myself bankrupt. I've lost everything, and I'm living in this dump.' He paused. 'I'd love to kill her, believe me. I'd love to get my hands round her throat and squeeze really tightly.' His hands mimed a throttling action, and he shook back and forth, the muscles in his arms flexing with built up tension. 'But I'm not the kind of person who'd threaten to do it first. I'd just do it.' He scratched at some red, lumpy welts on his neck. 'See! I've got hives now. I should be suing *her* for bloody emotional distress. I don't want to talk about her anymore.' And he slammed the door in my face.

I took the stairs back to the car park. Could it be Curtis? He was angry enough to do it, but he didn't strike me as the type of person who'd pussyfoot around sending the letters first, although the vigour of the throttling put a serious question mark over his head.

When I got to the Toyota, I examined it for new graffiti.

'I wish my wife was this dirty' was keyed into the dusty bonnet.

Still, at least they'd spelled it correctly, which was

something.

Hacker phoned as I made my way to Tracy White's house. 'Yo, I analyzed the handwriting from the threatening letters and the note Dr Spork gave you, and it's not a match. He didn't write them.'

'OK, cool, thanks.'

'And Brad just phoned in to say if you need him, his phone will be turned off for a while because he's going to Elstree Studios with Aleesha to film *Real Women,* and then onto some modelling shoot she's doing.'

'What sort of modelling shoot?' My stomach twisted at the thought of him seeing her naked. Even though he'd obviously seen her naked before, like most of the world, it didn't make it any better.

'I think she's doing a spread for *Playboy.*'

Yeah, 'spread' being the operative word. Good job I hadn't had any breakfast; I might've just thrown it up.

'Great,' I huffed.

I heard Tia's voice down in the background. 'When can I do the stakeout? Please, please, let me do it!'

I had to hand it to her; at least she was enthusiastic. 'Tell her I need to go and see Tracy first, then we'll know how many suspects we need to tail to see if they post anything.'

'Yo to that,' Hacker said.

I hung up and thought about what Curtis had said. It sounded like Aleesha had organized the sex video for publicity. Maybe Brad was right, and I should look closer to home. What if she really was sending the letters to herself to get her name splashed in the tabloids again? I could easily see her doing that. I tucked that thought into my frontal lobe for later and pulled up outside Tracy's flat in another rundown area.

Parking in the communal car park, I feared for the car's safety again. The places I was going lately, the Toyota would end up with the whole Urban Dictionary on it soon.

I dodged a rusty old child's bike in the corridor and knocked on Tracy's door. A little girl, about six with shiny ginger hair, opened it.

'Hi.' I waved. 'Is your mummy in?'

Her eyes grew huge. 'Are you from social services again?'

I smiled. 'No, sweetie.'

She shut the door again. A woman in her mid-thirties opened it a few minutes later. Her blonde hair was pulled up in a messy bun, and she had frown lines etched in her forehead.

'Yes? Can I help you?' she asked anxiously.

'Are you Tracy White?'

She nodded, frown lines deepening. 'Yes, who are you?'

'I'm Amber Fox. I'm investigating some threats that Aleesha's been getting.'

Her face flushed with anger. 'What's she accusing me of this time?'

'Nothing. But she's been getting some threatening letters.'

'You'd better come in.' She tilted her head inside the flat. 'So, someone's threatening her, are they?' Tracy sat down on a sofa. It sunk under her weight, as if all the stuffing had gone out. Her shoulders slumped like the stuffing had gone out of her, too. Her daughter stood next to Tracy, sucking her thumb and staring at me with big, innocent eyes.

Tracy patted her daughter on the arm. 'Go and play in your bedroom, darling. And stop sucking your thumb, you're getting too old.' Tracy gave her daughter a kiss on the head, and the little girl waved at me as she skipped out.

I sat down next to Tracy. 'Aleesha's been getting letters and other things in the post.'

'And you just assumed it was me, because of all that rubbish she said before about me stealing her phone?' She shook her head. 'Typical. Just blame the hired help.'

'I'm not assuming anything, Tracy.' I smiled. 'I just want to clear this up as quickly as possible.'

'I've got a criminal record for theft now because of her.' She rubbed at her forehead wearily. 'No one's going to hire me as a cleaner now, are they? And I haven't got any other skills.'

'There's no Mr White to help you out?'

She tutted. 'Not likely. He hasn't been around since Lisa was born.'

'Why don't you tell me what happened with Aleesha?'

'I told the police, and they didn't believe me.'

'So tell me. I'm listening.'

'Why should I trust you?' she said, but it wasn't in a nasty way. Just a dejected, 'sick-of-life's-knocks' kind of way.

I glanced around the flat. It was clean and tidy but cheaply decorated and sparse. Tracy's daughter seemed well cared for, but it was obvious social services had been round at least once to check on them. Tracy looked like a woman living below the poverty line and trying to make the best of a bad situation. If she wasn't the one threatening Aleesha, then I wanted to make sure she didn't get any more knock backs.

'I want to help, if I can,' I said.

She exhaled a tired sigh. 'I think Aleesha set the whole thing up for publicity. She knew I didn't have much money, and she knew my phone had stopped working, so she said she'd give me her old one. It was very out of character for her, because usually she just ignored me. She thought I was the lowly cleaner. It was Nathan who always gave me her lists of what she wanted cleaning that day.' She stared down at the threadbare carpet. 'Nathan was really sweet. He was always chatting to me while I worked and trying to get me to drink the horrible nettle tea he liked, or passing the day with some sort of chit chat, but she obviously thought she was above me.' She paused.

'Go on.'

'Well, anyway, I'd told Nathan about my mobile phone not working. It was only a cheap thing, but I don't have a home phone since I can't afford to pay for both. I couldn't afford a new phone, and I was worried about what would happen if Lisa had an accident or something and I needed to call an ambulance in the middle of the night. I think Aleesha must've overheard me. When I left that day, she said she had a few spare phones lying around that she didn't use, and did I want one.' Tracy shrugged. 'Well, of course, I said yes, please, and didn't think anything more about it. But the next thing I knew, there was a piece plastered in the press about me selling her text messages to the tabloids and trying to sell the phone on eBay.'

I frowned. 'So you didn't contact the press or put the phone up for sale?'

'No! I think she must've done it herself, but the police wouldn't believe me. Apparently, someone emailed *The Daily News,* saying they were me, giving them a list of all Aleesha's dirty text messages to various men. Someone had also set up an eBay account in my name from an anonymous Internet café and had the phone listed for sale. I don't even know how to use the Internet.' Her eyes welled up. 'The police arrested and charged me, but they said if I admitted it and gave the phone back, I wouldn't have to do any time, I'd just have a record.' She glanced towards Lisa's bedroom. 'I couldn't risk going through a trial, even if I was innocent. What if they tried to say I was an unfit mother and took Lisa away? Or what if I got banged up in prison? So, for a quiet life, I admitted it.'

'Did you confront Aleesha about it?' I remembered Aleesha had told me she'd also been arrested for hitting Tracy.

She bit her lip. 'I shouldn't have done, I know, but I was so angry. I mean, I hadn't done anything wrong. I went to the house and tried to ask her what was going on, and she started screeching at me. Then she literally flew at me, smacking me in the face and pushing me off the front step. Well, I wasn't having that. Not after everything she'd done, so I phoned the police that time and reported her. I had a massive black eye.'

'And what happened?'

'She was arrested for assault, but the police wouldn't file any charges. One rule for her and another for the likes of me, I suppose, since she's a *celebrity* and all.' She said the word 'celebrity' like it was a swear word.

I squeezed her hand. 'I'm sorry that happened to you.'

'Thanks. Not much I can do about it now, is there?' She sighed. 'I'm just trying to survive on the money I get from benefits at the moment, but it's not easy.'

'Well, if I hear of any cleaning jobs, I'll put in a good word for you.'

'Really? So you believe me?' Her face crumpled with gratitude.

'Yes.' Not only did I believe her, but I was building up a bigger picture of exactly the kind of things Aleesha stooped to for any kind of publicity she could get. Right about then, I wouldn't have minded killing her myself.

Chapter 9

My stomach rumbled with hunger as I left Tracy's place. Hurrah! My appetite was returning at last. Or maybe it was anger bubbling away inside me. Aleesha was a menace to society and didn't care who she stepped on to get her name in the papers. I was betting more and more that either Aleesha or Nathan sent the notes themselves. If she thought she could play havoc with innocent people for her own gain, then she had another thing coming. Knowing the way she operated, she'd probably blame it on some innocent person who would also end up with their lives ruined.

I realized I was near the mall and thought I could kill two birds with one stone. I'd get a progress report from Mum and Dad about whether anyone suspicious was buying chocolate knickers, and I could get my wedding night undies from Lace at the same time.

I parked up in the huge car park outside the mall and wandered past the shops. Riding the escalator up to the first floor, I thought about what to buy. A thong or lacy cheeky knickers. Ooh, maybe a basque? They would have to be cream-coloured, or else they'd show under the dress. I imagined Brad peeling them off me after the wedding. With his teeth. Yum. A slow grin spread across my lips.

Dad sat on a wooden bench outside the shop,

pretending to read the paper but really scanning who went in and out of Lace. Mum was inside, picking up bras and pretending to study them while checking out the chocolate knickers display.

I winked at Dad and strolled into the shop. It was underwear heaven. Bras, basques, thongs, knickers in all shapes, colours, and sizes. Plus, they had dress up outfits, like the French maid one Mum wanted, a leather Catwoman suit, and lots more. I wondered if they had a sexy Wonder Woman costume I could get.

'Amber! What are you doing here?' Mum put down the lacy bra she was holding and rushed over.

'I need some honeymoon undies.' I picked up a cream basque finished in lace and satin.

'So the wedding's still on? Only you had me a bit worried yesterday.'

I gritted my teeth, trying not to think what Brad was being subjected to at the *Playboy* shoot. 'Yes, of course it's still on.' I wandered over to some cream satin, cheeky knickers and picked them up, looking for my size.

'They're lovely.' Mum eyed them wistfully. 'Maybe I'll get a pair, too.'

I rolled my eyes.

'Try them on.' She nudged me with her elbow.

'Don't they get all funny if you try underwear on? Like if you try them, you have to buy them or something?' I stared at the knickers. They were pretty nice.

'Mmm, I think they do, actually.'

'So how do you know if they're going to fit? Usually, I just buy my knickers and don't bother, but these are special wedding knickers. I want them to be just right.'

'Good point.'

I shrugged. 'I know what to do.' And I pulled them on over my skinny jeans. Luckily, there were no security tags on them strategically placed to cause maximum discomfort, probably due to the fact they'd damage the delicate material.

I walked to the mirror, turned round, and examined my bum. OK, so the knickers over jeans wasn't the final look I was going for, but at least I knew if they fitted or not. And they did. Very snugly. Yep, my bum looked hot in them, if I do say so myself.

'What do you think?' I glanced at Mum.

She gave me a thumbs-up. 'They're lovely. Elegant and sexy.'

I nodded approvingly. 'Just what I was thinking. Now, what about a bra?' I turned my attention to the bras hanging on a rack above the knickers and picked out one that matched the bottoms. Satin with lacy straps and lace cups. I stroked my fingers over the material and imagined Brad's fingers doing the same with me in it. Perfect.

'Someone's at the chocolate knickers display,' Mum whispered. 'I'm going to keep my eye on them.'

I glanced up and didn't recognize the woman at the display as a possible suspect, so I studied the bras again, grabbing my size on a little glittery plastic hanger. I was heading to the tills to pay when some display bottles of perfume and body lotion caught my eye. I picked up a couple of pink perfume bottles and sprayed a tester on my wrist. Not bad. How about some body lotion, though? There were a couple to choose from. Vanilla Spice, Strawberry

Temptation, or Tantalizing Jasmine. Ooh, vanilla sounded nice. Very edible. Or lickable. The perfect honeymoon accompaniment. I grabbed the bottle and squeezed some on my finger, then rubbed it into my hand.

My skin got all hot and tingly. What kind of body lotion did that?

I peered at the bottle, which read, 'Vanilla Spice Edible Pleasure Gel'.

I quickly scanned the area to see if anyone had noticed me trying out pleasure gel in the middle of the shop, but luckily, no one had. I stashed the bottle back on the shelf out of pleasuring distance and headed to the checkout.

The sales woman was so busy security tagging some new stock at the till that she didn't notice me standing there for a while.

'Hi,' I said to get her attention, handing over the bra.

'Oh, I've got one of these bras.' She smiled. 'They're so comfy.'

I smiled back. 'It won't be on long enough to be comfy. It's for my honeymoon.'

'Congratulations!' She carefully wrapped up the underwear in some tissue paper and popped it in a glitzy bag before ringing up my purchase.

Handing over some cash, I thought it was definitely going to be money well spent.

'Have a great day!' She gave me my change and purchase and turned her attention back to the security tags.

Heading out the door, I waved goodbye to Mum, who gave me a horrified look.

Oh, crap. Mum must've seen me trying out

pleasure gel!

I cringed inwardly and, armed with my paper Lace bag, I strode out of the shop, avoiding her gaze. As I walked past Dad on the bench, his eyes widened when he saw me, his expression matching Mum's.

Ew, even worse, Dad must've seen me, too.

Double cringe.

Luckily, my stomach growling distracted me from dwelling on the huge embarrassment of being caught with pleasure gel in public. Even though I was a big girl and all that, it's not really the kind of thing you want your parents to know.

I'd hardly had anything to eat since Aleesha wormed her way into our lives yesterday, so I stopped off at Starbucks to get some caffeine supplies and a sugar injection. Three men already stood in the queue in front of me as I eyed the cake cabinet with new determination. A couple of workmen dressed in dirty overalls and fluorescent jackets came in behind me.

As I decided whether to have Death by Chocolate cake or cinnamon buns, the workmen laughed dirtily to each other.

'Bet she'd look good out of them, too,' one of them said.

'I wouldn't say no to that,' the other one said.

I felt their burning stares on me and turned round to give them a glare. How bloody rude. *I'm not deaf, you know!*

I drew my attention back to the cakes and carried on as the queue shuffled up towards the till. Hmm, maybe I should have a coconut macaroon. Coconuts are fruit, aren't they? That would be the healthy option.

I heard sniggers and whispered conversation in the seating area and looked behind me to see what was going on. Some people's eyes widened in a shocked look, some tried not to laugh, and some were downright staring at me. What was wrong with everyone today? Had the world gone mad? In my rush to get out of the house and get a move on, I hadn't brushed my hair, which probably made me look a bit like Dr Spork, but it wasn't *that* bad, surely. So why were they all looking at me?

'Yeah, I could just imagine ripping them off with my teeth,' one of the workmen said to the other, giving me a leering wink.

God, why are men so gross sometimes? I was about to give them an earful when Becky became free behind the counter.

'Hi, Amber. How's it going today?'

'Better, thanks.' I grinned and pointed at the cake display. 'Can I have four slices of Death by Chocolate cake, one of those healthy birdseed bars, two mochaccinos, and a sparkling water, please?'

'Coming right up.' She smiled, and then the smile fell off her face. 'Er…you do know you're wearing some satin lacy knickers over your jeans, don't you?'

Uh-oh! My eyelids pinged open as I looked down at the knickers.

Quick, think of something!

I faked a huge smile. 'Of course I know! Haven't you seen these new knickers-jeans on the catwalk this season? They're called jickers,' I said loudly, for the benefit of everyone staring. 'Yeah, they were designed by Posh—oh, sorry—VB, as she likes to be called now.' I nodded enthusiastically and shot a superior smile to the workmen. 'They're the new craze.' I gave Becky a nonchalant shrug. 'Everyone will be wearing them soon.'

Becky nodded approvingly at them. 'Yes, I think they look pretty cool, actually. Where did you get them? Only I haven't seen any like that in the shops before.'

'Er...' Bugger. 'Actually, Posh gave them to me,' I pretended to whisper, but really it was loud enough for everyone to hear.

A collective gasp spread round the seating area behind me.

'You know Posh?' Becky's jaw dropped open in awe.

'Uh-huh.' I put my finger and forefinger tight together. 'Posh and me are like that.'

'Wow.' Becky's mouth dropped open.

OK, so it was a bit of a white lie, but before the lying police get all hot around the collar, I had to do something to deflect the embarrassment.

'Anyway.' I leaned into the counter. 'I'm in a bit of a hurry at the moment. I need to give Posh a lift to go and see Umberto Fandango.'

'You know Umberto Fandango, the fashion designer, too?' Becky's jaw nearly hit the floor.

'Yep, he designed my wedding dress.' OK, that bit was true. And anyway, Umberto knew Posh, and I knew Umberto, so it wasn't such a wicked lie. Six degrees of separation and all that.

'Yes, right away!' Becky rushed off to get my order, and I glanced around the room with a smug smile.

Armed with sugar and coffee, I went back to Lace to explain my mistake and pay for the knickers, then headed back to the office. They were very good about it. Apparently, that wasn't the first time it had happened. See, it's not just me who gets herself into these things. And at least Mum and Dad hadn't caught me looking at the pleasure gel after all; they'd been trying to tell me I had the knickers on. Pheweee.

Tia's eyes lit up as I walked into Hi-Tec's reception. She clapped her hands together when she saw the cakes. 'Ooh, cake. Does that mean you're feeling better now?'

'Yep, and I'm on a mission.'

She jumped up and down. 'A mission to do the stakeout now? Can I, please? Can I, please?'

I laughed at her excitement. 'Let me call an office meeting, and we'll have a chat about it.'

'Cool! And then how about after the meeting we do that spell to solve the case?' Her eyes pleaded with me. 'Go on, it will work, I'm telling you.'

I shrugged and handed her a piece of cake. 'OK.' Why not? I needed all the help I could get. Plus, after hearing everything I had about Aleesha, I didn't want Brad or myself around her any longer than necessary. Who knew what she'd try to do to us?

I called Dad after I'd stuffed my face with two pieces of Death by Chocolate. 'Hey, Dad. I've got a new job for you. Can you come to the office?'

'No problem. Your mother's with me. She's really getting into it this stakeout thing. I think this could actually make our marriage stronger, you know. We can work together on the Neighbourhood Watch stuff now.'

'Great, bring Mum, too. I need all hands on deck.'

'We'll be there in ten minutes.' He hung up.

'What have you found out?' Hacker leaned back in his chair and laced his hands behind his head.

I handed over the healthy seed bar and sparkling water and told him what I'd learned that morning. 'I think there's a pretty good chance that Aleesha or Nathan could be sending the notes themselves, but I still need to cover other avenues. I don't think Tracy is involved, and now Dr Spork is out of the equation, too. I mean, I suppose he could've got someone else to write the notes for him, but I think he would've wanted to do them himself and give it the personal touch. And I'm pretty sure Jessie isn't involved, either. She's hurt and upset, yes, but she actually seems quite a sweet girl, and I don't really blame her for threatening to kill Aleesha at the studio. I think it was just a heat of the moment argument. Curtis is a possibility, and there's something about Felicia that makes me think she's up to something, too.'

Hacker let out a slow whistle. 'Aleesha sounds like a nasty piece of work.'

'She is.' I tapped my finger on the desk and thought about eating the last piece of Death by Chocolate cake. Maybe three pieces would be slightly piggish.

I dialled Brad's mobile, hoping to give him an update, too, but it was still switched off. Aleesha was probably still at the photo shoot. I curled a lip at the phone and sent a text so he'd get it when he turned his mobile back on.

'I think you were right. It's probably Aleesha or Nathan sending the letters. Keep an eye on them. But not too close! You might catch something!'

Ten minutes later, Tia brought Mum and Dad into the office, and they all sat down. Tia was practically bouncing off the walls at the thought of getting some investigative work to do. Mum chattered away with her about how amazing being on a stakeout at Lace was, and how she never knew it could be so exciting.

'I think I'm going to help your Dad out with the Neighbourhood Watch investigations from now on.' Mum beamed at me. 'That way, we can help solve crime *and* still spend time together.'

I didn't know if that was a good thing or a bad thing. 'Er…great. I think.'

'So, what's our mission?' Tia asked, eyes wide. Since she was dressed like Big Bird today, it was clear she couldn't keep tabs on Lace for chocolate knickers-buyers. She'd be spotted a mile off.

I told them all my theory about Aleesha sending herself the knickers and notes for publicity but said I still needed to cover all possible suspects. 'So, Tia, I need you to stakeout Aleesha's house and see if Nathan posts anything or does anything else suspicious. There's a spot just opposite from Aleesha's house where you can park. I think he may be still with Aleesha and Brad at the photo shoot, but when he gets back, make sure you follow him if he leaves the house.' I gave her the office file, and she memorized the details straight away. Tia was lucky to have a photographic memory.

'Fantabulous!' Tia's eyes lit up. 'I think we should all have code names.'

'What?' I asked.

'Well, you know, like in the films.'

'Yes, I agree,' Mum piped up. 'My code name can be Wonder Woman.'

'You can't be Wonder Woman,' I said.

She frowned. 'Why not?'

'Because I'm Wonder Woman. I've even got the knickers.' They weren't the big, original ones that came up to your belly button, either. These were a variety of different sexy ones with Wonder Woman logos and designs.

'That's not fair.' Mum's shoulders slumped. 'I always wanted to be Wonder Woman. You can be Red Fox instead.'

I sighed. Beam me up, Scotty.

'I can be Penelope Pitstop!' Tia shrieked.

Hacker gave me a sympathetic smile. Dad just shrugged.

'Well, who am I going to be, if I can't be Wonder Woman?' Mum gave me an eye-roll. She taught me all I know about eye rolling, and if eye rolling were an Olympic sport, she'd win gold every time.

'Oh, for God's sake, we don't need code names,' I said.

'Well, if Tia's Penelope Pitstop, I want one, too,' Mum said. 'OK, I'll be Catwoman. I saw a really nice Catwoman outfit in Lace.'

'Fine!' I threw my hands in the air. 'Right. Mum, can you carry on staking out Lace, just in case?' I handed her a photo of Nathan and Aleesha that Hacker had printed off the Internet. I didn't think Aleesha would be buying the knickers herself. She was too easily recognizable, but maybe she could sneak out wearing some sort of disguise.

'I'm not Mum, I'm Catwoman.' Mum took the photo and nodded vigorously. 'Affirmative. That's a Ten-four, big buddy.'

It was my turn to roll my eyes. I was good at it, too. At the very least, I'd get a silver medal.

'What? Isn't that what you say to confirm you've

received the mission instructions?' Mum asked. She'd obviously watched way too much TV. 'Plus, I can get some more chocolate knickers today while I'm working. After you left, they just put them on sale!' Mum's eyes lit up, and she raised an eyebrow at Dad.

Oh, Goddy, God.

'Dad?' I said, but he was too busy giving Mum a knowing grin and thinking about the chocolate knickers to notice me. 'Earth to Dad!'

'Pardon? Did you say something?' He tore his gaze away from Mum and looked at me.

What was wrong with them all? They seemed obsessed by these bloody chocolate knickers and sex. Maybe I was just jealous because I wasn't getting any, with Brad being away. And I seriously hoped Brad wasn't getting any, either. I shook my head to tune out the green-eyed monster again.

'Dad, I need you to stakeout Curtis and see if he posts any packages.' I gave him Curtis's address.

'Received and understood,' he said, suddenly all business.

'Hacker, I'll need you here in case I have any technical stuff to be done, and I need to follow Felicia.'

'Shouldn't we synchronize watches?' Tia asked.

'Why?' I asked.

'Well, duh! That's what they always do in the spy films.'

'Oh, yeah, good idea,' Mum agreed.

Tia looked at her watch, then said to Mum, 'What time do you have?'

Uh-oh. Was this a good idea, letting them work on the case? When I investigated the disappearance of

106

Tia's Dad, Tia had blown up a washing machine and a warehouse. OK, maybe I was a teensy bit responsible for the warehouse, but the washing machine was all down to her. I studied Mum and Tia warily as they fiddled with their watches. Well, Brad wasn't here, and it wasn't as if I had much choice of back up to use, was it? They would just have to do. Although I was pretty sure I'd end up needing psychiatric help soon.

'So, we all know what we're doing?' I glared at Tia and Mum.

Nods all round.

'Great.' I stood up and grabbed my rucksack.

'Aren't you eating that cake?' Tia pointed to the last piece on my desk.

'No, why, do you want it?'

'I think we can use it for the spell.' She eyed it with excitement.

'How could a piece of chocolate cake possibly help me solve this case?'

'Well, I need something that you've touched in the last half an hour, and the case involves chocolate knickers, so I think the chocolate could make the spell more powerful. Come on.' She grabbed my arm in one hand and the cake in the other, propelling me down the hallway to the empty conference room. 'Let's go in here. We won't be disturbed.' She practically shoved me through the door, and it swung shut behind us.

'Look, are you sure this is a good idea? You know what happened the last time I did one of your spells.'

Tia glared at me. 'It will work, trust me.'

'Uh-huh,' I said in a disbelieving tone. 'I don't really have time to do the spell now.' I turned round

107

and reached for the door handle.

'But you promised. You can't back out now.' Tia chewed on her lip, not wanting to meet my gaze. 'And...you absolutely have to do it. Right this minute.'

'Why do I have to?'

'Er...Because you do.'

One hand flew to my hip, and I tilted my head, trying to catch her gaze. 'What do you know? Have you been getting a psychic premonition thingy?'

Her big blue eyes met mine, a frown creasing her forehead. 'Yep.'

I made urgent sweeping gestures with my hand for her to spit it out. 'Well, what can you see?'

'That's the thing. I can't actually *see* anything.'

'Then what are you talking about?'

'It's just a feeling I'm getting.' Tia was back on the lip chewing again.

I sighed. 'And what can you *feel*?'

'Something bad is going to happen between Aleesha and Brad,' she blurted out quickly, before she could change her mind. 'And we need to do the spell to stop whatever it is from happening.'

My eyes narrowed. 'Bad as is in he's going to sleep with her?'

Tia did a nervous stretching thing with her mouth that made her look like a frog. 'I don't know. I just know it's bad.'

I started pacing the floor. 'Well, what other kind of bad can there be?'

'Maybe I shouldn't have told you. But I thought you'd want to know.'

Even though I knew Aleesha didn't seem to have any moral codes, deep down I did trust Brad. Maybe

108

it was pre-wedding jitters making me extra nervous that he was spending time with her. Or maybe it was because I also knew that even people who seemed to have the strongest relationships could be swayed. I couldn't take any chances. Not when Brad and I had overcome so much to get back to this point again.

I stopped pacing and swung round to face her. 'Quick. Let's do the spell!'

After putting the cake on the large conference table in the middle of the room, Tia pushed me down into one of the leather chairs. 'Sit.'

I saluted her. 'Sir, yes, sir!'

She did the glare thing again. 'You have to take this seriously, otherwise it won't work properly.'

I stared at the ceiling, wondering if I was just having a very peculiar dream and not, in fact, about to do a spell with a piece of stupid cake. Was it just me, or did this sound totally ridiculous?

Tia took a pen and a piece of paper from the stack in a drawer under the table and thrust it at me. 'Right. Because the spell is about Aleesha, you have to write her name in the middle of the paper.'

OK, that seemed harmless. I scrawled Aleesha's name as instructed.

'Now, fold the paper up and rest it on top of the cake.'

I did as she said. 'Then what do we do?'

'Touch the cake.' She jerked her head towards it.

'With any particular body part?'

Humongous glare. 'You're just being crazy now.'

And a spell with cake wasn't crazy? 'Well, I don't know!'

'Put your hands out and touch the cake lightly with your fingers. Then close your eyes and imagine that

109

you've already solved the case, and Aleesha never contacts you or Brad again.'

'What? This all sounds ridiculous.'

I got a hand on hip for that.

I sighed and gave in, closing my eyes, trying to visualize what she'd said.

My first thought was how moist the cake felt, and that when this was over, I wouldn't mind smearing Brad in it and licking it off. I hadn't really spent any time with him in the last couple of days, and I was in serious need of a body-licking session. Oh, yeah, that was another reason why I probably couldn't be a nun. I don't think body-licking is allowed. A smile curved up the corners of my lips as I imagined Brad on the—

'Are you focusing?' Tia shrieked in my ear, making me jump and knocking me out of my fantasy.

'Yes!' I squeezed all sexy thoughts of Brad out of my mind and thought about solving the case and catching the suspect immediately. Then I imagined Aleesha shipwrecked on a desert island in the middle of nowhere, with no phones or Internet, and never messing with anyone's lives again.

'OK, now open your eyes and rip the paper into four pieces,' Tia said.

I licked my fingers to get rid of the chocolate residue, tore the paper into four, and left it on the table. Then I waited for something to break or catch fire as it normally did.

Nothing happened. Phew.

'That's it!' Tia beamed at me.

'Nothing happened. Nothing broke.' I grinned back. 'That's a first.'

'See, I told you this is going to work. By tonight, I bet you'll have solved the case, and you and Brad will be back at home together all snuggly wuggly.'

I raised an eyebrow. Brad was a roughty toughty ex-SAS guy. Somehow, I didn't think 'snugly wuggly' was in his vocabulary, but hey ho. At home with Brad on our own sounded good to me. I took the cake. I'd put it in the fridge to use on him later.

Chapter 10

I drove to Elstree Studios and parked outside the entrance, scooching down in the car so I wouldn't be seen while I waited for Felicia to leave. The only problem was that the Toyota would be easily recognizable with graffiti scrawled across it, but I had to hope Felicia wouldn't notice.

Tom Baker was in the guard booth again. He reached into a packet of sweets and popped one in his mouth. I pulled out the binoculars from my rucksack and zoomed in on the packet. Jelly Baby Buses. I knew it! It definitely was him.

After an hour, I glanced at the dashboard clock. Six p.m. Hopefully she'd be finished soon. I jigged my foot up and down and adjusted my ass in the seat, since it had started to fall asleep. Stakeouts were so boring.

My phone buzzed with a text from Mum.

'Catwoman to Red Fox! Nothing interesting going on at Lace, and they've now closed. Bought four more pairs of chocolate ones. Vegas will be fun!'

I groaned as the phone buzzed again with another text, this time from Tia.

'Penelope Pitstop to Red Fox! Brad and Aleesha just arrived back at house with Nathan. This is soooo super cool! Can I get an ejector seat fitted to my car?'

I figured she was joking, so I didn't reply. Turned

112

out she wasn't.

'Can I? I just Googled ejector seats on my phone, and you can get one done at specialist garages. Love Penelope Pitstop xx'

I texted back.

'Stop looking at Google and watch out for Nathan leaving. No ejector seat!! They give you whiplash and make all your teeth fall out from the G-force.'

'How about smoke bombs fitted to the exhaust? That way I can disappear in a puff of smoke if someone follows me.'

'Just watch Nathan!'

'Meanie!'

At half past six, Felicia's car came out of the gates. She waved goodbye to Tom and drove off down the road. I put the Toyota into gear and followed her a few car lengths behind. Forty-five minutes later, she pulled up on the driveway of her parents' vicarage. A tall man dressed in black, wearing a white vicar's collar, opened the door as she was about to put the key in the lock. He pointed to his watch and frowned. She shook her head slightly in return, and her hair swished about. Maybe her parents were strict. I wondered what they'd think of her having a crush on Steve.

As I waited for something amazingly exciting to happen, my mobile rang.

'Hey, Foxy,' Brad drawled. Instantly, I wished I wasn't sitting in a graffitied Toyota on the outskirts of town and was instead in a delicious bubble bath with my hubby-to-be.

'Hey, yourself. How was your day?' That twinge of jealousy tugged at my insides again. It was irrational and stupid, I knew that. Brad had never given me a reason to doubt his faithfulness, but unfortunately feelings weren't always logical, were they?

'Awful. I took Aleesha and Nathan to the studios to film *Real Women*. You should see the way she treats people. She's a nightmare.'

'That's pretty much what everyone says about her.' I fought the urge to have another dig about how he'd ended up sleeping with her.

'Then we went to the *Playboy* shoot, which involved Aleesha wearing lots of sticky silver glitter body paint and nothing else.'

The twinge got stronger at the thought of him seeing another woman naked. 'Hmph.You didn't have to look!'

'I'm supposed to be acting as her bodyguard. Of course I have to look.'

'I suppose,' I said sulkily.

'I got your text. So, you think this could just be a big publicity stunt by Aleesha as well, do you?'

'I wouldn't put it past her.' I gave him an update on what I'd found out so far. 'She's a conniving home-wrecker who likes to manipulate people. What did you see in her?' OK, I couldn't resist.

'Well, I was lonely. And drunk. And it was at a party, and it was a heat of the moment thing.'

'You? You don't get lonely.'

'Well, a man has needs, you know. And you wouldn't speak to me, let alone see me. It was a long time after you ended things.'

'Actually, you ended things when you buggered off and didn't tell me where you were for months,' I snapped.

'We're not having this conversation again, are

114

we?'

I sighed. I was sick of this conversation, too. We were over it. We were back together. We were getting married. That was all that mattered. 'No. Let's have a weddingy conversation instead. I bought my wedding underwear today.'

'Why? It won't be on you long enough. You might as well go commando.'

'I can't wait for this case to be over. I still need to get a manicure and a bikini wax. When am I going to have time? You're not going to like a hairy bride, are you?'

'I'd still love you even if you were the hairiest woman on earth.'

I laughed. 'What have you and Aleesha got planned tonight?'

'She wants to play Scrabble.'

I snorted. 'What, naked, dirty word Scrabble?'

'Who knows? I just can't wait to get out of here.'

Good. 'Well, I've got a date with a French man.'

There was silence for a few seconds. 'Look, nothing is going on with Aleesha and me, I swear. This is strictly business.'

'Relax. It's Mr Cabernet Sauvignon.' I smiled to myself. 'Marmalade and French Men are my only company now.'

'Foxy, Nathan's just left the house this minute. Have you got anyone watching him?'

'Tia.'

'Oh. Is that a good idea?'

'Well, she's enthusiastic, I'll give her that. And it's not like we've got much choice. You're with Aleesha, and I need this case solved so we can just relax and look forward to the wedding.'

'I can't wait. Especially for the after-wedding commando part.' His voice was low, primal.

My after-wedding parts sprang to attention at the sexy tone in his voice. 'Mmm.' I grinned and noticed Felicia open her front door and walk down her path. 'Ooh, gotta go, Felicia's on the move.'

'Later.' He hung up.

Felicia swung a left, heading towards the end of the road. I pulled on a baseball cap, tucked up my hair underneath it, and put on a pair of big sunglasses, then got out of the car. On the opposite side of the road, I tailed her with my head down. What was she up to?

It didn't take me long to find out. As she turned into the next street, she walked up to a post box, took a small brown Jiffy bag out of her coat pocket, and dumped it in the box. As she scurried back to her house, I waited until she was a good distance away before heading back to the car. So, was mousey little Felicia sending the letters? The Jiffy bag looked remarkably similar to the ones Aleesha was getting. Or was she posting something innocent? Like a present for a friend? Or maybe her Dad ran a Bible delivery service in his spare time. Only one way to find out. I needed to get into that post box. It was too late for the Post Office to collect the mail that night, so I had until early tomorrow morning to get into it.

Brad was the best lock picker in town, but since he was out of action, I'd have to get Hacker to help me open the box. I picked up the phone to ring him and it buzzed with an incoming text from Tia.

'Red Fox, Nathan's on the move. Following! Yipppeee. Over and out. Penelope xx'

116

I shook my head and dialled Hacker. 'Yo. How are you at breaking into post boxes?'

'Never tried, but if I can break into Saddam Hussein's palace, I can break into a post box.'

My jaw dropped open. 'You were at Saddam Hussein's palace?'

'My lips are sealed.'

'Spoil sport.'

'What's the address of the post box?'

I told him the street name. 'How are we going to break into it?' I thought about the heavy cast iron red cylinder. There was a lock at the front, but I suspected it would be hard to get into.

'Post boxes have a brass security lock on the inside with more than six thousand possible combinations. There's no skeleton key, so each box has an individual one. I'll need to hack into the Post Office system and get the key details, then I'll make one up on my laser cutter.'

'You have a laser cutter? I bet you've got a missile launcher stashed away somewhere, too, haven't you?'

'Funny you should say that. Anyway, it might take me a while. If the post is safe for the night, you don't need to hang around. I'll call you when I'm on my way, and you can meet me there. It's probably best to do it in the early hours of the morning when everyone's asleep.

'Gotcha.' I hung up, and my phone immediately buzzed with a text from Tia.

'Nathan now at the supermarket, buying melons, cucumbers, and nettle tea. Chocolate doughnuts are on special offer at the moment for your info!'

I threw the phone on my passenger seat and tapped

my very real, unmanicured nails on the steering wheel. It was eight p.m., and I had hours to kill before we got into that box. It looked like me getting cosy with the French man was out of the question tonight. I'm sure my liver breathed a hefty sigh of relief.

I took off in the direction of my still empty home to wait. Even if Brad wasn't there to give me cuddles, I could get Marmalade to oblige.

As I pulled up on the driveway in front of the barn conversion, my lights caught something on the front step. Oh, crap. I hoped Marmalade hadn't brought me another present.

I got out of the car and approached the step, groaning. What would it be this time? A mangled rabbit? A chewed-up mouse?

Bugger, it was worse.

A packet of chocolate knickers with a folded up note underneath greeted me.

I glanced around the darkness, wondering if Dr Spork was lurking in the bushes, waiting to jump on me and slide a ring on my finger, but no one was around.

I slid the note from underneath the knickers and read it:

'I know you love me, too, Amber. Stop denying it. I've got some new knickers for you, as the other ones have probably melted when you wore them for me last night. The Sporkites told me we should have a simple wedding with just family and friends. How does the 18th suit you?

Love you always

Dr Spork xxx'

Great. Just great. I picked up the knickers and went

inside the house, then phoned Suzy.

'Yes?' she answered.

'Good evening, my wonderful sister, how are you?' I dumped my rucksack on the floor and the knickers in the bin in the kitchen.

'What do you want?'

'Dr Spork's sent me more knickers.'

She sighed.

'OK, so I get that you can't do lobotomies and electric shock stuff, but how about putting him in a padded cell? You said yourself that erotomanics can become dangerous.'

'A padded cell? Don't be ridiculous.'

Me, ridiculous? I wasn't the one sending knickers to people!

'The Sporkites are peaceful creatures. They wouldn't tell Dr Spork to harm you.'

See what I mean about psychiatrists sounding like their patients? 'Are you listening to yourself? Do you actually believe in Sporkites, Suzy?'

'Of course not,' she snapped. 'But it's what *he* believes. This is just a harmless fixation on you.'

'Well, give him some double treatments, or up his medication, or something.' I huffed. It had been a long day, and I really wasn't in the mood for dealing with nutters who sent me knickers.

'I have a double appointment with him tomorrow that will last three hours. I'll make sure we work extra hard, OK? Satisfied?'

'Well, I suppose I'll have to be.' I hung up. If I ever did need to see a psychiatrist, it definitely wouldn't be Suzy.

Marmalade strolled into the kitchen, nudging his head against my leg. 'Meow.'

'What? Does that mean you want food again?'

'Meow.'

I picked him up, gave him a cuddle, and then fed him. While he chowed down, I phoned Tia and Dad. I told them about Felicia and the suspicious package she'd sent, and called off their surveillance for the night. It had to be Felicia sending the knickers and threats. It just had to be. And once I could prove it, case closed. I'd go back to my happy life with Brad, and Aleesha could find someone else to harass. Maybe Tia's spell was working after all.

Pacing up and down the living room, I waited for Hacker to call. I gave up at one a.m. and turned on the TV. Tania Tate and another comedian were hosting a twenty-four-hour live *Children in Need* show with loads of different celebrities doing all kinds of things on air to raise money for charity. I watched singers and bands performing various acts, famous actors doing a celebrity bake-off with each other, a well-known comedian interviewing Lady Gaga, and some soap stars going head to head at *Strictly Come Dancing*. At quarter past three in the morning, Hacker rang and told me to meet him at the post box.

When I turned up, he was already parked in his black Range Rover. I left my car a little way down the street and walked to him.

'You made up a key?' I whispered as he got out of the Range Rover carrying a large hessian sack.

'Yep.'

We glanced around the dark street. Luckily, this was a nice neighbourhood, and everyone was tucked up in their beds in snoozeland. The post box was at the end of the street, and the two nearest streetlamps weren't working. Handy. Hopefully, we wouldn't be seen.

'Did you mess with the streetlamps?' I asked Hacker

He grinned, and his gold front teeth glinted in the moonlight. 'Of course.'

We walked in silence to the post box. I stood guard and kept a lookout while Hacker inserted his special key into the lock.

I held my breath and waited.

He turned the key, and I heard a metallic click before the door opened. We didn't want to get caught going through the contents there and then, so Hacker quickly shovelled all the post into the sack and locked up the box again.

'Meet me at the office,' Hacker said.

I nodded and jogged back to the Toyota, then followed Hacker down the deserted streets for the half hour trip back to Hi-Tec.

He carried the heavy sack into the office effortlessly and dumped the contents on the conference room table.

'That's a lot of post.' I stared at the big mound, wondering how many dodgy things were posted every day throughout the whole world.

We pulled on some latex gloves and examined every Jiffy bag in silence, concentrating on the task at hand. Luckily, there weren't that many amongst all the envelopes, and at half past four, I hit the jackpot.

'Got it!' I waved the Jiffy bag addressed to Aleesha in my hand, a huge smile plastered all over my face.

Hacker stretched his arms over his head. 'Good. I

never want to see another envelope as long as I live.'

I carefully undid the flap and looked inside, pulling out a letter and a packet of chocolate knickers. The letter said:

'Die bitch! I will make you pay for everything!'

'Felicia has a unique way with words.' Hacker read it over my shoulder.

'I wonder if she writes poetry, too.' I grinned. 'Well, well, well. Not only does meek and mild, daughter-of-a-vicar have a potty mouth, she's also making death threats. I'm sure the man upstairs wouldn't like that very much.' I slipped the Jiffy envelope into a clear plastic bag and put it in my rucksack for evidence.

'At least you can wrap the case up now and get Brad away from Aleesha.'

My grin widened. 'Yep. Bubble bath and chocolate cake coming up!' I allowed myself a quick fantasy before reaching for my mobile and calling Brad. It rang and rang and went to voicemail.

Why wasn't he answering? It was almost five in the morning, for God's sake! A horrible stab of jealousy poked me in the heart as I imagined him and Aleesha tangled in her sheets, smearing jam over each other and having a mutual licking-fest. Seriously icky.

I left a terse message. 'Call me when you get this!' And I stabbed the *end call* button. 'Why isn't he answering the phone?'

Hacker looked uncomfortable. 'Maybe he's turned it to mute while he's asleep.'

'Yes, but he never does that. Ever.'

'Maybe the phone's faulty and the ring tone doesn't work.'

122

'Hardly likely.'

'I don't know, but I do know he loves you so much he'd never cheat on you.'

Of course he did. Didn't he?

'Look, why don't you go home and get a couple of hours sleep while I go and put the letters back in the post box before it gets light. There's not much you can do about Felicia until later this morning.'

I tried to ignore the queasy feeling in my stomach about what Brad was doing, and exactly why he wasn't answering the phone in the early hours of the morning.

I drove home and fell into bed, exhausted, but when I woke up three hours later, the duvet was tangled around my legs and the bottom sheet was all skewiff, like I'd been tossing and turning. I had a severe headache, too. Probably stress. Or maybe the Death by Chocolate cake was off.

Marmalade pounced on the bed and sat on my head, padding at my hair.

'Hey, boy. How are you?'

He purred in return.

'Do you think Brad slept with Aleesha last night? Meow once for "yes" and twice for "no".' I picked him up and put him on my stomach, staring at him with baited breath. What? Seriously, Marmalade was an intelligent cat.

He blinked at me. 'Meeeeeeooooooow.'

I sat up in bed, dislodging him. 'Wait, was that one meow or two rolled into one?'

'Me,' he said.

'What does that mean? Is that half a meow, in which case it means yes and the other half would mean no?'

Marmalade burped. I didn't even want to contemplate what that meant. Usually, he was really accurate. I put him on the floor and threw the covers back. Right, there was only one thing to do. This called for my Wonder Woman knickers.

I grabbed a pair of red, blue, and gold cheeky knickers with white stars on the back and 'Wonder Woman' written on the front. If Aleesha was trying to entice my man, I'd put up a serious fight. I shimmied into some skinny jeans, UGG boots, and a tight black long-sleeve top. I thought about shoving some tissue paper down my bra to increase the C cups but decided against it. The shift in gravity might make me fall over. I tipped my head upside down and ran fingers through my curly waves to calm down the bed head.

Ooh, bad idea. My head throbbed so hard it felt like it had a herd of stampeding wildebeest in there. I swiped on loads of mascara and pink lippy and looked in the mirror.

There. I was as pretty as Aleesha any day. And it was all real. Plus, I didn't have to show the whole world everything, either! I gave the mirror an attitude head bob and headed downstairs to make coffee. Today, I was going to confront Felicia, and that would be the end of that. She'd stop sending the letters and maybe get some psychiatric help (not Suzy's), and Brad would be back with me. Here. Where he belonged.

Marmalade stared up at me with longing as I turned the kettle on to boil. I grabbed a tin of tuna from the cupboard and popped the lid open. When he smelled the equivalent of feline heaven instead of his pongy cat biscuits, he went nutso. He meowed and rubbed his head against my leg.

'OK, I need to get a straight answer out of you before you get the tuna.' I wasn't above a spot of bribery to get info out of my cat.

He sat down and gave me a bug-eyed look.

'Did Brad sleep with Aleesha last night? You know the drill, meow once for "yes" and twice for "no".'

'Me Meow.'

'Urgh!' I groaned. 'What was that? Two meows or one and a half? What does one and a half even mean? And why aren't you talking sense today?' I scraped the tuna into his bowl, and he wolfed it down as I made coffee. My appetite had vamoosed again through worrying about Brad and Aleesha. Good job I'd packed in lots of Death by Chocolate yesterday to make up for it.

As I sipped away, my mobile rang. It was Brad. The coffee started gurgling away in my stomach. What was he going to say? *Sorry, I missed your call last night, I was shagging Aleesha* or *Sorry, I had my phone on mute and I didn't hear it?*

'Hello, Brad,' I said tersely. 'What were you doing in the early hours of this morning that made you miss my call?'

'Aleesha's dead.' Tension oozed from his voice.

Chapter 11

'What do you mean, dead? How could she be dead? You're her bodyguard?' I gripped the phone and rested on a stool at the breakfast bar.

'Yes, but I wasn't sleeping in the same room as her.'

My heart breathed a sigh of relief about that. 'So, what happened, then?'

'I was drugged. So was Nathan. The only thing I can think of is there was something in the nettle tea, which both Nathan and I drank last night. I remember Nathan making the tea, and he took his up to bed with him. I made sure the house was secured and alarmed and then drank mine sitting at the kitchen table. The next thing I know, it's morning. I'm still asleep at the table, and Nathan's waking me up looking like a zombie and telling me to come quick, because Aleesha's dead.'

'How did she die?'

'Strangled. With a pair of chocolate knickers.'

Uh-oh. Death by chocolate. My thoughts drifted back to Tia's spell with the Death by Chocolate cake.

Fuckity fuck. Had I caused this by accident because I was imagining Aleesha out of our lives? Nah. Not possible.

But was it? When the daughter of a famous voodoo high priestess had gone missing recently, I'd

126

investigated the case and been slap bang in the middle of some dodgy black magic. I was convinced that a voodoo spell had given Brad meningitis. He'd nearly died, then. What if I was responsible for her death?

'Oops,' I said, a huge guilt cloud settling on my shoulders.

'"Oops" wasn't the kind of response I was expecting.'

'I think it was me. It was the Death by Chocolate and the desert island that did it.'

'Foxy, you're not making any sense.'

'Well, that happens a lot.'

'Why "oops"?'

I told him about the spell.

I pictured him rolling his eyes at me. He didn't believe in that mumbo jumbo, and I had to admit I didn't really. Sort of. Well, maybeish. I mean, how did you explain the voodoo and meningitis thing?

'Are you rolling your eyes at me? That's my job.'

'It wasn't anything to do with a spell. Someone—a person, not a spell—murdered her in her bedroom after drugging Nathan and me.'

'Right.' But I wasn't convinced.

'And it's my fault.' His voice hardened with regret. 'I was supposed to be her bodyguard, and I failed.'

'Yes, but how could you guard her when she was asleep? You have to sleep, too. And you couldn't sleep *with* her.' Part of me felt really bad then. I was pleased that he hadn't been sleeping in the same room as her, but at the same time, she was dead because of it. Now I felt doubly guilty.

'I know, but maybe I should've had Hacker or one

of my other ex-SAS team here doing a split shift with me, so there would always be one person on duty.'

I pictured him running his hand over his hair with worry.

'To be honest,' he carried on, 'I didn't take the threats as seriously as I should have. I really believed she was doing it to herself, and when I got your text last night and you thought the same thing, I kind of relaxed my vigil. I made a bad judgement call, and now she's dead.'

'It's not your fault. You didn't kill her.'

'No, but I didn't protect her, either.' Guilt and anger and something else I couldn't quite work out filtered through his voice.

'How did the killer get in?'

'The alarm system was off when Nathan woke me up, and I know I'd turned it on before I had the tea last night. I got Hacker to do a check, and he said the system hadn't been hacked into. It was disabled at the source here in the house. There's no sign of forced entry anywhere, so either someone was an expert at breaking and entering, or someone had a key and knowledge of the alarm code.'

'Have you called the police?'

'Yes. Romeo's on his way. I don't think he was too happy to hear from me.'

Great. Even though it had been a while since Romeo and I had split up, I'd still broken his heart. I still felt guilty about it, and I wasn't really looking forward to rubbing his nose in the fact that I was now getting married to Brad. Wow, the guilt was just stacking up today.

'Well, I found the person sending the knickers and

threatening letters.' I told him about Felicia, but something niggled at my brain. 'If it was Felicia who killed Aleesha, why send her a letter the day before she's going to do it? It doesn't make any sense.'

'It sounds like she's severely unbalanced, so anything's possible. Maybe it was a spur of the moment thing. Maybe she decided to kill her in the middle of the night after she'd sent the letter.'

I had my doubts about that. Grabbing my car keys, I said, 'I'm on my way over. I'll be there soon.'

'OK.'

I rang Dad and Tia to give them an update, telling them not to bother with their stakeout duties anymore, and drove to Aleesha's turquoise beast.

The Scenes of Crime Officers were already there when I arrived, going through the house armed with fingerprint powder, cameras, and evidence bags. Romeo was in the kitchen, leaning against the kitchen worktop with his arms folded, looking very pissed off. Brad sat at the kitchen table we'd sat at before, looking tired. If you didn't know him, you'd think he was calm and collected as usual, but I could see the haunted look of guilt and anger in his eyes. Nathan sat next to Brad, who was the same shade as a clammy piece of cod. His eyes were red, and his eyeliner was smudged halfway down his cheeks. He held a balled up soggy tissue.

'Hi,' I said to everyone.

'Amber.' Romeo's face softened and he gave me a gorgeous smile, his hazel eyes lighting up like he'd missed me.

There it was again; the guilt doing a flip-flop in my belly. He looked well. I hoped he was moving on with his life. I hoped he'd found someone who loved him like he deserved.

'I can't believe she's been killed!' Nathan's hands flew to his spiky hair, and he wailed dramatically. He forgot he was holding the tissue, and blobs of it fell off into his hair. 'What am I going to do without her? She's all the family I've got left!'

Brad's gaze cut from Nathan to me.

'Are you OK?' I put my arms round Brad's shoulders, kissing him on the lips. I felt bad about doing it in front of Romeo, but I couldn't hold back.

Brad kissed me back. Hard. God, I'd missed him.

'I'm OK,' Brad said. 'I don't know what the drug was in that tea, but the SOCOs have taken blood samples from Nathan and me. It was something pretty strong, although it seems to have worn off now.'

I smiled, grateful that there seemed to be no long-lasting effects. Brad was like an ox. It would take a lot to put him out of action permanently, but it could've been worse. What if the person who drugged them had used something lethal instead?

'I was just telling Romeo about what you'd found out so far, and how Felicia was the one sending the threats,' Brad said as I sat down next to him.

Nathan jumped up from the table, pointing his finger accusingly at Romeo. 'What are you hanging around here for? Arrest this Felicia woman now! She's the one who killed Aleesha.' Tears streamed down his face.

'We don't know that yet,' Romeo said. 'I'm just trying to find out what happened here. Let's go over it again, starting with the events yesterday, so I can get this clear in my mind.'

Nathan wiped his eyes.

'I took Aleesha and Nathan to Elstree Studios to film *Real Women* at midday,' Brad said. 'We were there for two hours, then we all left to go to a photo shoot for *Playboy* in the afternoon. They took photos of Aleesha covered from head to toe in silver glitter paint for about three and half hours, and we all got back here about six-thirty.'

'I went out to the supermarket after we got back,' Nathan squeaked in a high-pitched voice, wiping his eyes. 'Then when I came back, I made dinner, and we watched some DVDs and stuff. Before we went to bed, I made some herbal tea for Brad and me. I took mine to bed with me, but I must've fallen asleep before I even finished the whole lot. Brad drank his here, at the kitchen table, and that's where I found him this morning, still passed out. When I woke up about eight, the first thing I did was go into…' Nathan's lower lip trembled, and he pressed a hand to his chest. 'Oh, my God, this is so terrible.' He fanned his face. 'I went into Aleesha's room to wake her up, she's dreadful for oversleeping, and I…f…f…found her! The herbal tea must've been drugged. How else can you explain us both being knocked out?' Nathan leaned his elbows on the table, tugging at his short blonde spikes.

'What sort of herbal tea?' Suspicion laced Romeo's voice.

'Not herbal as in drugs! It was nettle tea.' Nathan pointed to a canister of loose tealeaves on the kitchen worktop. 'You can inspect them if you want to prove it.'

'We'll need to take it away and get it analyzed for whatever drugs were allegedly in it, anyway. What else happened?'

'While Nathan was making dinner last night, Aleesha had a shower to try and get the glitter body paint off, but some of the stuff was so thick and sticky it wouldn't all come off,' Brad said. 'At around midnight, when Nathan was making the tea, she said she was going for a bath and then heading for bed.'

Nathan took a huge sniff and wiped his nose with the tissue before reaching for another one from a box on the table. 'She was lying on the bed with the knickers wrapped round her throat when I found her. Her eyes were open, staring lifelessly back at me. It was horrible! I screamed as I ran down the stairs. ' He threw his arms on the table and crumpled forward onto them, sobbing hard.

'Did either of you touch the body?' Romeo asked.

Nathan look up, horrified, his mouth flapping open. 'No. I couldn't touch a dead body!'

'I went upstairs after Nathan woke me up this morning and looked from the doorway of her bedroom,' Brad said. 'As Nathan told you, her eyes were wide open. Her skin was also waxy and pale, and rigor mortis was setting in. I've seen enough dead bodies in my time to know it was obvious there was nothing we could do for her, so I didn't need to touch her.'

'I don't think it was Felicia who did this,' I said.

'Of course it must be,' Nathan said. 'She was the one threatening Aleesha with death. You said she sent the letters. Who else could it be?'

I told Romeo about the letter Hacker and I had got from the post box. 'Your guys can fingerprint it.' I reached into my rucksack, grabbed the plastic bag I'd put it in, and handed the letter over. 'But I still

132

don't see why she'd send a letter the night before she was going to kill her.'

'Maybe she didn't think about doing it until later that night, after she'd sent it,' Brad said.

Romeo shrugged. 'Seems unlikely to me.'

And I had my doubts about that, too. I suspected Felicia had led a sheltered, strict life, what with her Dad being a vicar. Was she really capable of murder? Was she an expert in picking locks and cracking alarm codes? I doubted it. Then again, she'd sent letters threatening to kill someone. That wasn't exactly Christian-like and innocent, was it?

'She's obviously crazy!' Nathan squealed. 'And crazy people don't do rational things, do they?'

'I agree, but I still can't see Felicia doing this,' I said.

'If she sent death threats, she could be capable of killing her,' Romeo said. 'Although, I'm with Amber on this. Why send a letter the night before she's going to kill her? That doesn't sit right with me.'

And if it wasn't Felicia, who was it?

'Did you change the locks after the incident with Tracy White?' I asked Nathan. 'She would've had access to the house as a cleaner.'

Nathan pressed his hands to his forehead, thinking.

Could it have been Tracy? She had reason to, but somehow she didn't strike me as desperate enough to kill Aleesha in revenge for how she'd been treated. I remembered Curtis wanting to strangle Aleesha. Now, him I could see doing it. And since Dad stopped his stakeout after we found the letter from Felicia, he could've popped out in the middle of the night and done it. He'd been in the house before. He could've noticed the alarm code while he was here or swiped Aleesha's key to take a copy.

Nathan gave a huge sniff and wiped his eyes with the tissue. More blobs disintegrated and stuck to his day-old mascara. He looked like he'd been stuck in a snow globe for a week. 'Yes, we did change the locks after that. But Aleesha was always leaving her bag on set with her keys in it when she went to the studio or photo shoots. I've lost count of the times she lost her bag on set and accused people of stealing it, only for it to turn up in the dressing room or in the kitchen later on.' He tilted his head.

'Actually, it's possible anyone could've stolen her keys from her bag. She never really used them, because most of the time I was here to let her in, or I was with her and used my keys to get into the house.'

'Check to see if her keys are still in her bag,' Romeo said to Nathan.

Nathan leaped to his feet. 'Now, where did she put her bag?' He glanced around the kitchen, his face red and puffy from crying.

'Is it a turquoise Dolce & Gabbana one?' I spied it on the floor and pointed.

Nathan picked up the bag and dumped the contents out on the kitchen table. He rummaged through lipsticks, a mobile phone, a diary, a packet of tissues, receipts, mascara, a bottle of perfume, and some super-sized Tampax.

Nathan glanced up at us as he picked up a key ring with a bunch of keys on it. 'They're still here.'

'So, either someone took her keys from her bag without her noticing, copied them, and put them back later, or they picked the locks to get in,' Brad said. 'But what about the alarm code? I set it before I drank the tea. Whoever got in would have to know that, too.'

Nathan wiped his eyes. 'I don't know. We always changed the code whenever Aleesha dumped the man in her life, just in case any of the exes were bitter with her for ending their relationship.'

'When was the last time the alarm code was changed?' Romeo asked.

'Er…' Nathan rubbed a hand across his forehead. 'About two weeks ago. After she split up with Stig. Then she was seeing Steve for a while, and after that Alfonso, but neither of the relationships lasted long, and they never came to the house, so it wasn't changed again.'

Romeo jotted that down in his notebook. 'OK, we'll run the tests on the tea to see if any drugs were used to knock you out. But it's very strange that the killer knew you'd both drink the tea and be out of action all night.'

My thoughts exactly. Was Nathan as innocent as he was making out? Maybe he wasn't as distraught as he seemed. He could just be a very good actor. He knew exactly what the alarm code was. Maybe he'd told someone. Or perhaps he staged it so he could bump Aleesha off and inherit from her. This whole thing screamed of an inside job.

'Who was Aleesha's heir?' I asked.

'Well…me.' Nathan gasped. 'What are you trying to say? That I killed her?'

'We're not saying anything yet, until we have some evidence,' Romeo said.

'But…but…' Nathan stuttered as he tried to get his words out. 'Whenever I accompany Aleesha to the studio or on a job, everyone knows I drink a cup of herbal tea while she's filming *Real Women*, and they know I have another one just before bedtime. I'm always talking to people on set about the benefits of nettle tea, you see. It's really good to keep you regular. I've never been constipated since I started drinking it.'

'And who else had access to the tea?' I asked. 'How would they be able to slip drugs in it without you noticing?'

'Well, I always leave the tin in the studio kitchen next door to the set so people can help themselves. Someone could easily have slipped drugs into it without me knowing.' His face crumpled. 'Oh, God, I thought I was just spreading the nettle love around, and now it looks like my tea got her killed,' he shrieked. 'If we were awake, we could've stopped it!'

'OK, so a lot of people might've known about your tea drinking habits, but who knew Brad would drink the stuff, too?' I thought how convenient that was if it was an inside job.

His eyelids shot open. 'I don't know! Maybe they didn't know he was here, too. Maybe it was just a coincidence.'

I guessed it could've happened like that, but I didn't believe in coincidences. Something was definitely off.

Romeo looked thoughtfully between Brad and Nathan. 'You were both here when it happened, but both of you say you were conveniently drugged. Someone allegedly got into the property with no sign of forced entry, and now suddenly Aleesha is dead. That seems to point to one of you.'

'It must be Felicia!' Nathan reached for another tissue as tears streaked down his face and landed on the table.

'Hey.' Brad held his hands in the air, palms up, facing Romeo. 'I had nothing to do with her death. It shouldn't have happened. It was my fault I wasn't guarding her properly, and I feel guilty as hell about it. But if Aleesha left her keys all over the place, anyone could've made a copy. Or picked the locks, like Amber said. And maybe they guessed the alarm code. Felicia would've had access to Aleesha's bag with her keys at the studio *and* Nathan's tea.'

Romeo uncrossed his arms, strode over to Brad, and peered at his hands. 'So what's that on your hand, then?'

'What?' Brad turned his palms and examined them.

I peered over, too. Silver glitter was smudged on the tip of his right index finger, and on the edge of his palm was the tiniest amount of something brown. Something that looked suspiciously like melted chocolate.

A frown creased Brad's forehead, and his eyes flashed with something I couldn't read.

'I don't know what it is or how it got there, but it definitely wasn't on my hand before. I did *not* kill Aleesha.' Brad stared at Romeo, his eyes darkening. 'I'll have to live with the fact that I was responsible for not guarding her efficiently, but I did not kill her.'

'You said you didn't touch the body.' Romeo narrowed his eyes at Brad. 'But you've got silver glitter and what looks like chocolate stains on your hand, which is highly suspicious. When I examined

Aleesha's body, she still had glitter around her neck, along with melted chocolate stains from the knickers.'

'Romeo, that's ridiculous!' I spluttered. 'Brad was protecting Aleesha, not trying to kill her.'

'Well, he didn't do a very good job, did he? Let's see what the evidence says, shall we?' Romeo called for one of the SOCO teams to come into the kitchen.

Nathan burst into tears again. His face paled, and he fled from the room, shrieking, 'I can't take this. I don't want to be the same room as the killer.'

'I'm not your guy,' Brad said to Romeo, his voice edged with determination. 'I don't know how that got on my hands. I didn't touch Aleesha at all. Maybe the *real* killer put it there when I was drugged to frame me.'

As the woman from SOCO collected the substances on Brad's hands with a swab and placed them in individual plastic bags, my eyes met Brad's.

Something lurked beneath the surface, and I couldn't tell what. Anger? Annoyance at being accused of killing Aleesha? Worry? Or guilt? And if it was guilt, was that just because he hadn't done his job properly, or because he'd actually killed her? What really happened here last night?

I swallowed a lump in my throat as a horrible feeling fluttered around inside. This was ridiculous. Brad couldn't have killed Aleesha.

But I knew Brad had killed before. When I was investigating a case involving gangland boss Vinnie Dawson, I'd been kidnapped by Vinnie and his cronies. Brad had killed to save my life then and got rid of the body with his ex-SAS friends. I was pretty sure Brad had killed David Leonard, too, who was an ex member of Brad's SAS unit and had killed Brad's business partner, Mike Cross. And that was without all the secret SAS stuff he'd never told me about. Just how well did I really know Brad?

But then another thought popped into my head. This was the man I was going to marry, for God's sake. I knew him. I knew his morals. He would never kill someone just for the sake of it. And what possible reason could he have for killing Aleesha? Unless...unless they were involved in a relationship that had gone wrong.

'I'm going to have to arrest you until we can analyze what's on your hands.' Romeo stared at Brad.

I leaped from the chair so hard it fell over. 'Romeo, you don't seriously think Brad did this, do you?'

Romeo took a step closer to Brad. 'I know you killed Vinnie Dawson, even though we never found the body. And I know you killed David Leonard, even though there was no proof. I know you're more than capable. And so far, all the evidence is pointing to you.'

'What about Felicia?' I said.

'A minute ago you didn't think Felicia had killed her,' Romeo said. 'All of a sudden, when Brad becomes a possible suspect, you think she did it?'

'No! I don't think Felicia killed her.' I threw my hands in the air. 'But I know Brad didn't, either.'

'How do you know? Were you here last night?'

'No.'

'Exactly, and the evidence looks like he was in very close contact with her, even though he claims he wasn't. Close enough to strangle her.' Romeo gave Brad a steely look, and a crackle of tension between them permeated the air.

Brad rose from the chair slowly and faced Romeo. 'If I had killed Aleesha, you can bet that there wouldn't be any evidence left lying around.' His eyes flashed with anger.

My heart danced around in my chest as I stood in between them. 'This is crazy!' I said to Romeo. I looked frantically from one to the other, not quite believing this was happening.

'Brad Beckett, I'm arresting you on suspicion of murder. You do not have to say anything, but it may harm your defence if you do not mention, when questioned, something you later rely on in court. Anything you do say may be given in evidence.' Romeo pulled handcuffs out of his pocket. 'Are you going to give me any problems?' Romeo sized Brad up. He knew Brad was trained to kill and could take him out with one quick move if he wanted to.

'Romeo!' I stood silent for a moment as I tried to process the unbelievable situation unfolding before my eyes.

'Don't worry, Amber. I didn't do it. While I'm at the station, find out what really happened.' Brad turned round and held his hands out behind him for Romeo to cuff him.

My eyes burned with anger and helplessness, my temperature gauge reaching boiling point. Romeo called one of his colleagues to put Brad in the police car and take him to the station.

'What are you doing?' I asked Romeo after Brad was led out of the house. 'Is this about us? Are you still upset with me?'

He studied me for a while before saying, 'No. This

isn't about us. This is about evidence that points to Brad.'

But maybe it was about us. I'd broken Romeo's heart, I knew that. Was he so jealous I was marrying Brad, he'd stoop to this? Was he prepared to do anything he could to stop the wedding from happening? I didn't think so. Romeo was a good guy. He was the best, and I knew from working with him for so many years that he was a great police officer, but he was wrong about Brad. He had to be.

'Just how well do you really know him?' Romeo's gaze nailed me to the spot.

'I know him,' I said, with more conviction than I actually felt. My mind was all over the place, doubts and niggles and fears creeping in. 'And I know he wouldn't have done this.'

'You know, I always wondered about Brad's business partner getting killed like that. Mike Cross put up most of the money for Hi-Tec, and then suddenly he dies and it all goes to Brad. Pretty lucky for Brad, wasn't it?'

My forehead pinched in anger. 'Mike was killed by David Leonard, who went crazy after he got out of the SAS and started killing members of his old unit. You know that as well as I do.'

'You were the lead police officer on the investigation. I've only got your word to go by.' He raised a suspicious eyebrow. 'So, I'll say it again. How well do you really know him?' He paused, scrutinizing me.

I glanced away.

He gripped my forearm. 'Strangulation is a crime of passion, you know.'

'I'm aware of that.' I shook my arm away and ran

a hand through my hair. 'What about Felicia? She sent the letters; she threatened to kill Aleesha. She must be your prime suspect. And Curtis, and the other people who had a motive for killing her. Are you going to be speaking to them, or have you just got your sights set on Brad for some bizarre reason?'

'I wouldn't be doing my job if I didn't bring them in for questioning, too. I'll need to arrest Felicia for the threats to kill anyway.'

'Well, while you're doing your job, I'm going to do mine and find out what really happened. I'll prove Brad didn't do this.'

Wouldn't I?

Chapter 12

I drove to Hi-Tec with my hands shaking so much it was hard to control the steering wheel. It couldn't be Brad, it just couldn't. And yet...how did you explain the glitter and chocolate on his hands? What if they'd slept with each other and something had gone wrong? Like Romeo said, strangulation could be a crime of passion. Maybe Aleesha had wound Brad up or said the wrong thing. In the heat of the moment, he'd snapped and killed her. It was possible. I knew from all my years on the police force that anything was possible.

Then I mentally kicked myself for having doubts about him. There had to be a rational explanation why substances from Aleesha's body were on Brad's hands. And if it wasn't Brad, who really had killed her?

Maybe this was all a dream. I was really tucked up at home in bed having a horrible nightmare, wasn't I? Yes, that was it. It couldn't be real, could it? I pinched myself to check I was really awake.

Ouch! Shit. It wasn't a dream. It was a very scary reality.

I parked the Toyota in Hi-Tec's car park at a messy angle and ran up the stairs to the office.

Tia stood behind the reception desk looking like...well, I wasn't quite sure. She wore a purple jumpsuit with squiggly pink, yellow, and orange lines all over it. My eyes went squiggly to match the lines.

'Hey, Amber! I know how much you liked the Death by Chocolate cake, so I bought you some more.' She held up a slice of cake on a plate.

'Don't talk to me about Death by Chocolate cake,' I said through gritted teeth. 'I never want to see chocolate again! That stupid spell killed Aleesha.'

She put the cake on the desk and shot round to me. 'What are you talking about? A spell can't kill someone.'

'Oh, yeah? What about the voodoo curse that gave Brad meningitis?'

She gasped. 'OK, maybe you're right. But as long as you did the spell exactly how I said, it should've worked.'

'Well, it didn't. Aleesha's dead, and Brad's been arrested for her murder.' I stomped down the hallway to the office I shared with Hacker, guilt welling up in the pit of my stomach again that somehow this was all my fault. But I'd only imagined Brad smothered in Death by Chocolate cake, not causing Aleesha's death by chocolate knickers.

I threw my rucksack on my desk so hard it bounced off and landed on the floor. I kicked it halfway across the room.

Hacker jumped to his feet. 'What's going on?'

'Aleesha's been murdered, and Brad's been arrested.' I flopped down onto the chair.

'What?' Hacker's voice rose with disbelief. 'What happened?'

So I told him.

'That doesn't sound good.' Tia bit her lip as she

144

sat on the edge of my desk.

'That's an understatement.'

She put her arm round me and patted my back.

'We need to find out who the real killer is and quick,' I said to Hacker, as thoughts of my wedding in five days took a nose-dive out of the nearest window.

'What do you need?' Hacker asked, his forehead pinched in a frown.

'I think it's too convenient that Nathan and Brad were both drugged in the house at the same time. Look closer into Nathan's background. I want to know why a twenty-nine-year old guy would want to live with his sister. Also, find out if any of the suspects had experience with any kind of electrics or security systems. Someone knew how to get into that alarm system, and it was state of the art.'

Hacker turned to one of his computer screens.

'What can I do?' Tia asked.

I pressed my fingers to my temples, feeling the throbbing from earlier returning with vengeance. 'Can you get me a really strong mochaccino and a couple of headache tablets, please?'

She bobbed her head up and down. 'I'm on it. Want some chocolate muffins, too?'

I growled.

'OK, no chocolate. Sorry, I forgot.' She rushed out the door.

'We need to find some evidence of who was in Aleesha's house,' I said to Hacker. 'If it wasn't Nathan that did it, it's got to be Felicia after all.' I thought I shouldn't have dismissed her before. 'I didn't think it sounded plausible for Felicia to post a letter the night before she kills Aleesha, because

145

Aleesha would never get it, but I guess that doesn't mean she didn't do it. If she could send threatening letters, she's not exactly stable and thinking rationally, is she? The trouble is, Felicia lives with her parents, and I don't know how to get all of them out of the house so I can do a search.' I tapped my fingers on the desk, trying to come up with a plan.

I picked up my mobile and phoned Dad, giving him a quick version of what had happened.

'Brad wouldn't have done that,' Dad said. 'No way.'

'I know.' Didn't I? So why did I still have a niggling doubt? 'My bet is either Felicia or Nathan, but I don't have time to wait around. I think we need to check out the other suspects and see if some kind of evidence leads them to the murder, too. Can you stakeout Curtis's flat again. When he leaves, break in and get a good look around. You need to check clothes, surfaces, and bathrooms for any traces of silver body glitter or chocolate from the knickers. Some of it would've transferred onto the killer.'

'Of course. Anything to help Brad. What about Tracy's place? Do you want me to do that, too?'

'Would you mind?' I asked. Even though I didn't think Tracy had anything to do with this, maybe she did. I didn't know what to think anymore. My brain was scrambled, and everything I thought I knew was all topsy-turvy. The only thing I did know for certain was that I couldn't wait around to eliminate one suspect before going after the next. I had to try to blast them all at once so I could find something, anything, which would get Brad off the hook and out of a possible life sentence. I had to feel like I was doing *something* to help.

'Of course I don't mind. Can't have my future son-in-law being accused of murder, can I?'

I drew in a sharp breath as the morning took its toll on me.

'Don't worry, Amber. It will be OK,' Dad said.

'Uh-huh.' But I didn't know if anything would be OK ever again. My whole life had come crashing down around me.

'I'll let you know as soon as I've found something,' Dad said.

'Thanks.' I hung up as Tia came back bearing mochaccinos from Starbucks and a sparkling water for Hacker. I downed half of mine in one gulp after swallowing the headache tablets.

'I'm going to do another spell to correct the last one,' Tia said to me and rushed off.

'No!' I yelled after her. 'Don't do anymore spells!' But she was gone.

I groaned, dreading the thought of what would happen now. Crap.

Hacker took a swig of water and sat back in his chair. 'OK, here's some background info that might help. Aleesha and Nathan's parents were pretty wealthy. They died in a car accident when Aleesha was twenty and Nathan was eighteen and left them a couple of million pounds each. Aleesha became the new "It Girl" on the scene and was out partying with the other rich and famous socialites every night. Nathan joined in, too. It looks like Aleesha also invested her money well, and then her career took off and she was worth a small fortune. But Nathan developed a big spending habit. He liked flashy cars, designer gear, and fancy holidays. Only, he was spending way beyond his means. His money ran out a few years back, and he had to sell his house and cars to pay off his debts. He was pretty much broke, apart from what Aleesha gave him in salary. That's why he lived with her.'

'Interesting.' I raised an eyebrow, hoping things were slipping into place. 'As Aleesha's only heir, then, Nathan had several million reasons to bump her off.'

Hacker nodded. 'Looks that way. But also, Dr Spork has been living on incapacity benefits because of his delusional disorder and erotomania, so he didn't work. *But* before he developed his mental health problems, he was an electronics engineer and then a game software designer. He was working for some big software company, designing a game called Sporkville, when he had a nervous breakdown. With his background, though, he'd know all about computer codes and electronics. I already know Aleesha's alarm system wasn't hacked. The alarm was disabled at the house, so Dr Spork could've tampered with the wiring system to get in. Just because Dr Spork didn't write the letters, doesn't mean he didn't kill her.'

'Maybe Felicia and Dr Spork were in on it together.' I leaned forward, feeling an idea brewing. 'Or maybe the letters gave Nathan the perfect cover.' My brain had a mental light bulb moment. 'Yes. Someone starts sending Aleesha letters threatening to kill her, so Nathan gets the idea in his head he can bump her off for the inheritance, and it will get blamed on the stalker who's sending the letters and knickers.'

'Sounds plausible.'

I downed the rest of my coffee. 'Well, Aleesha's

house is swarming with police and SOCO at the moment. Plus Nathan's there, so I can't go in and get a good look round yet to see if there's any evidence that points to him.' I jigged my knee up and down impatiently.

My mobile rang as I tapped my fingernails on the desk.

'Hey, Amber,' Romeo said, his voice deadly serious.

'Hi.' I leaped to my feet and paced the office. 'What's happening?'

'I just thought you'd like to know that the toxicology results came back on Nathan and Brad's blood tests.

'Yes?' I said breathlessly.

'They both contained very high levels of sleeping drugs and tranquilizers. Enough to knock someone out for hours.'

'See! I told you Brad was telling the truth.' Except that now messed up my theory about Nathan. Unless Nathan drugged Brad, killed Aleesha, and then drugged himself afterwards to make it look like they were both out of action.

'I don't think Brad's telling the truth,' Romeo said. 'He could easily have drugged Nathan, killed Aleesha, and then taken the drug himself as an alibi.'

Damn. Bloody crapping damn. It worked both ways, didn't it? Except...'Romeo, you know as well as me that if Brad had killed her, he wouldn't have left any evidence.'

'Maybe he got sloppy in his old age. Maybe they were having an affair and he killed her in the heat of passion. How else do you explain the substances on his hand?'

I stopped pacing, feeling the anger rising and something else...doubt. 'He wasn't involved with her in that way. It was a business relationship.' But I knew Aleesha wouldn't stop when she had her sights set on something, and it was obvious she'd had a thing for Brad. Had Brad betrayed me with her? 'Has SOCO analyzed the swabs from Brad's hands yet?'

'No, we're still waiting for the results. Felicia's been arrested for sending the death threat letters, and she's down at the station now with her parents. I'll be questioning her shortly.'

'Right. Well, can you let me know as soon as you get an update, please?' I said stiffly.

'Yes. Oh, and Amber. I'm just doing my job, you know. This isn't anything personal.'

'Uh-huh.' I let my tone speak for itself. I hung up and turned to Hacker. 'Right, Felicia's parents' house is empty. Can you give me a hand to search it while they're all at the station?'

'Sure thing.'

Hacker and I drove in silence, which was pretty rare for me. Usually, my mouth worked overtime, but I was exhausted with worry, lack of sleep, and lack of food. I was determined to find out what really happened to Aleesha, but part of me was freaking out that I didn't want to know. Because what if it really was Brad?

I tried to shake the thought away, but it hovered over me like a doomsday cloud.

It was eleven a.m. and the street was quiet. Part of me didn't even care if we got caught, but the other part knew it wouldn't do any good to be banged up in a cell next to Brad for breaking and entering when I had to be out here, trying to find a clue.

'Drive round the back,' I said to Hacker. 'I'm pretty sure these houses back onto a playing field. We might be able to get in from there without being seen.'

Hacker obliged, and we parked up in front of a scout hut. There was only one other car there. In the distance, an elderly woman walked her dog on an empty football pitch.

'We should wait for her to leave,' Hacker said.

'I don't know how much time we have.' I bit my lip, willing the woman to go away.

After five minutes of throwing a ball for her retriever, she made her way leisurely back towards her car.

'Hurry up! Don't you know we've got houses to break into!' I said.

'We look suspicious, just sitting here in the car,' Hacker said as she got closer. 'Kiss me.'

'What?' My eyebrows shot up to my hairline.

'It will look like we're a couple who's parked up for a bit of romance.'

I groaned. 'OK, but no tongues. And never, ever speak of this again.' I leaned over and pressed my lips to his, my gaze looking over his shoulder as the woman opened the rear door of her car and let the dog jump in.'

'As e one et?' Hacker asked, his lips pressed firmly to mine muffling his words.

'O.'

The woman got in the driver's seat and started the engine, fiddling with the radio.

'Ome on!' I said, still stuck in a lip-lock with

Hacker.

Finally, she drove off and we broke apart.

'Right, let's go.' I was out the door and running to Felicia's six-foot wooden fence that backed onto the playing field.

Hacker gave me a leg up, and I climbed over and into the garden before he hoisted himself up. We ran to the back of the detached 1980s house devoid of any nice architecture. Patio doors opened into the lounge, and a door led into a kitchen. The kitchen door looked easier to get into.

We pulled on some latex gloves before Hacker got a lock-picking tool out of his pocket, exactly the same as the one Brad had, and fiddled around in the door lock.

'Right, you start downstairs, I'll start in Felicia's bedroom,' I said. 'Look for traces of anything that might link her to Aleesha's murder, but especially on clothes. If Aleesha still had glitter on her from the photo shoot, tiny specks of it are bound to have got onto the killer's clothes. And the chocolate. Some of it would've melted from the heat of the killer's hands when she was strangled with the knickers.' I pushed away thoughts of the stains on Brad's hands.

I padded up the navy blue-carpeted stairs and poked my head in the first bedroom. A simple wrought iron double bed and fitted wardrobes sat along one wall. A pair of men's slippers lay on the floor next to one side of the bed. Some curlers rested on top of a bedside table on the other. It must be her parents' room. A large wooden cross hung on one wall, with a picture of Jesus above the bed. I was betting Felicia's mum and dad's sex life was non-existent. Who could get into the throes of passion with Jesus watching?

After searching and finding nothing incriminating, I ducked out and up the hallway into a bathroom. A plastic laundry hamper in the corner caught my eye. I opened the lid and rummaged through the dirty clothes. I'd done some strange things to solve cases in my time, but rummaging through dirty underwear and stuff wasn't my idea of fun.

I pulled out men's trousers, cardigans, and Y-fronts (yuck), and threw them on the floor, turning my attention to the women's clothes. What had Felicia been wearing when I'd tailed her yesterday, and would she have worn the same clothes last night?

Picking up skirts, ladies' trousers, and dresses, I inspected each one for signs of glitter or chocolate.

Nothing. Not even a mini chocolate speck.

I let out a huge sigh, put everything back in the basket, and examined the sink and bath. If Felicia took a shower when she got back, there would probably be traces of glitter somewhere. Even the smallest speck lodged somewhere around a tap or on a plug would be proof. I pulled a mini Maglite out of my back pocket and shone it around the taps and down the plugholes, but no glitter sparkled back at me.

Opening the door opposite the bathroom, I found myself in a stark and impersonal bedroom, painted white with a single bed in the corner, covered by a white duvet. A cheap dressing table sat underneath the window. A mirrored fitted wardrobe ran the length of one wall. The other walls were bare except for a picture of God. At least I thought it must be God, although I've never met him so it could've been someone entirely different. It was a man with long white hair, a long white beard, and long white robe in the middle of some floaty clouds. You know the drill. A Bible was on the floor next to the bed. I didn't think God would be too impressed at Felicia threatening to kill someone, but I could be wrong. Weren't there lots of fanatical religious people who committed horrible crimes in the name of religion? Had Felicia taken things a step further and carried out her threats to kill because she thought Aleesha was a threat to society's morals?

I opened the wardrobes and examined her clothes carefully but couldn't see anything that would tie her to Aleesha's murder. I searched the rest of the room and ditto.

I ran back down the stairs and found Hacker poking around in the under stairs cupboard, checking jackets, coats, and shoes.

'Find anything?' I asked hopefully.

'No. You?'

'Nah.'

I glanced in the kitchen. It had a washing machine but no dryer. 'There's no recent washing hanging up to dry upstairs, anything down here?'

'No.'

'So it looks like Felicia didn't wash her clothes from last night then, unless she got rid of them somewhere else, and every other thing I've looked at had no traces of glitter or chocolate. Maybe she's only responsible for sending the letters.'

'Looks like it. I haven't found anything that could possibly connect her to Aleesha's murder.' Hacker hung the last jacket back on the hook. 'Ready to leave?'

I nodded and felt the doomsday cloud move with me. One suspect eliminated. How many more before it led back to Brad?

Chapter 13

'Any luck with Curtis's or Tracy's place?' I asked Dad on the phone as we drove away from the scout hut.

'I got into Tracy's when she took Lisa to school. It's clean, although I've got some really nice graffiti on my car that says, "Some people do this for fun. I'm just a knob". I'm still staking out Curtis's bedsit, but his car's here and the curtains are closed.'

'Maybe the curtains are closed because he had a busy night killing Aleesha.'

'Oh, wait. A couple of detectives just turned up on his doorstep. I used to work with one of them in CID.'

'OK, stay on the line and tell me what happens.' I picked up a pen and doodled angry slashes on a piece of paper.

'Curtis has opened the door. The police are going in.'

The slashes turned into big zigzags. I bet Suzy would have a field day working out what that meant.

'What now?' I asked Dad urgently.

'No sign of them yet. Wait! They're coming back out.'

'That was quick.'

'They're going to the next door neighbour's bedsit. A woman in her mid-twenties just opened the door. The police are talking to her.'

I doodled so hard I ripped the paper to shreds. I balled it up and threw it in the bin before attacking another piece. It was quite therapeutic.

'The neighbour's nodding a lot and pointing to Curtis's bedsit,' Dad carried on his commentary.

What did the woman next door have to do with it? I wondered what Curtis had told them. I wished, not for the first time, that I had a super power to turn me invisible so I could listen to conversations without people knowing.

'The police are leaving now. One of them is on the phone to someone.'

'OK, great, Dad. Let me know what happens.' I hung up and dialled Suzy to find out what time Dr Spork's mega appointment was so I could get into his flat and poke around. I wasn't going to leave any stone unturned.

'I don't have much time,' Suzy answered brusquely.

'Hello to you, too.'

'What do you want? I'm rushed off my feet this morning with back-to-back consultations. I bet you'd like to know that I phoned Dr Spork last night, and he's admitted his erotomanic fixation on you. Now, I'm confident I'll be able to treat him successfully with some in-depth sessions. Admission and realization is the first step to being cured.'

'Good. What time's his appointment?'

'This afternoon. Four p.m. Why?'

'Oh, nothing. Thanks.' I hung up and glanced at Hacker. 'Dr Spork will be out of his place at four. We need to check it out then.'

'OK.'

Did Dr Spork kill Aleesha after all? He obviously

had a giant secret stash of chocolate knickers, and as an electronics expert, he could easily have disabled the alarm.

I spent the next few hours like a nervous ball of energy, spending my time pacing the office, fidgeting, or doodling. At three p.m. Romeo phoned.

'What's happening?' I asked.

He paused for a second, and I knew it couldn't be good news. 'Curtis has an alibi. Some colleagues spoke to him, and he was with the woman next door until nine this morning. He couldn't have killed Aleesha.'

'You're sure?' My voice jumped up a notch. 'He couldn't have slipped out unnoticed during the night at any point?'

'The woman is very sure. She said he kept her pretty active all night long.'

'Well, I hope for his sake he didn't do a video of it this time,' I snapped. Another suspect bit the dust. 'How do you know she's not lying to protect him?'

'The woman's also a police informant, so she's well known to us. Her information has always been reliable. She's got no reason to lie about this, Amber.' He paused for a beat. 'And there's something else. The lab did a rush job on the substances found on Brad's hand. They're a match to the chocolate from the knickers used to strangle Aleesha, and the remains of the glitter found around her neck. I'm sorry.'

My legs turned wobbly, and the room swam before my eyes. This couldn't be right. Brad couldn't have killed her. I put my hand on my desk to steady myself, trying to fight down a rising wave of nausea and panic. My cheeks burned with anger, and something else. Fear.

'We've just charged him with Aleesha's murder. Felicia admitted sending the letters but denies murdering her. She said she was in love with Steve and trying to rid the world of immoral behaviour.'

'Well, she's got a funny way of going about it. How do you know for certain it wasn't her that killed Aleesha, too?'

'She's got a watertight alibi. She was volunteering at an all-night soup kitchen for the homeless. I've got five other people who worked with her saying she didn't leave the building from eleven p.m. until eight this morning. The pathologist puts Aleesha's time of death at three a.m., so there's no way Felicia killed her.'

'No. No, no, no.' I flopped onto the chair, all my blood pooling to my feet. 'You're wrong,' I said, but it came out more like a question.

'The evidence says otherwise.' His voice softened.

'Is Brad still in the cells?'

'Yes. His court hearing is tomorrow morning. The crown prosecution service will be asking for Brad to be remanded in custody with no possibility of bail before the trial.'

'Can I see him?' I managed to croak.

'You can see him tomorrow morning before court. He'll need you to bring him a suit, since the clothes he was wearing were taken for evidence.'

'Oh, God.'

'I'm really sorry.'

I dropped the phone in my lap as my world spun around in front of my eyes.

Hacker's arms circled round me. 'What's happened with Brad?'

'They've charged him with murder,' I managed to squeak.

'You know he didn't do it, right?' He took my chin in his fingers and tilted my face up to meet his gaze.

'I don't know. I don't know anything anymore.'

He held onto my shoulders firmly, staring deep into my eyes. 'I've known Brad for a long time. I trust him with my life. He wouldn't just snap and kill someone for the sake of it. He's the most controlled person I know. He's only ever killed for a good reason.'

'Yes, that's the thing, though. I know he's killed for Queen and country in the SAS. I know he shot Vinnie Dawson to save my life. And I know he executed David Leonard to get a serial killer off the streets. I know he would only kill someone with good reason. But what if there *was* a reason for killing her? There are lots of things he's never told me about what went on in the SAS. I know he's not allowed to, and I don't want to know most of it. But I know what he's capable of.'

'What possible reason could there be for him to have killed her?'

Tears sprang into my eyes. 'What if Brad still fancied her and slept with her? What if he got angry or jealous with her about something and it got out of control? How do you explain the substances on Brad's hands?'

'He was framed,' Hacker said, slowly and clearly so there could be no possible mistake. 'Are you listening to yourself?' His nostrils flared with frustration. 'You know how much he loves you. He'd never cheat on you.'

'I thought I knew, but I don't know what to believe

anymore.' I glanced away, not wanting to meet his penetrating eyes. Brad's and my life as we knew it had just come crashing down around our ears. We couldn't lose each other now. We just couldn't.

'So, what? You're just going to give up on him? Believe what they're saying? Because I don't believe it. Not for a second.'

'No, I'm not giving up. I want to know for sure. I'm going to eliminate all the suspects and see what we're left with.'

He pulled me to my feet. 'Come on. It's half-past three. Let's go and search Dr Spork's place.' Leading me past the reception, I looked over at Tia.

Her hands flew to her cheeks, knowing something was wrong. 'Omigod, what's happened now?'

'Brad's been charged with murder.' Tears pricked my eyes.

Do not cry, Amber. You're no good to anyone if you fall apart.

I sniffed and wiped my eyes on the back of my hand as Tia came round the desk and hugged me. 'What can I do to help? I've already done the spell, and things should be back...' She trailed off when she caught my look.

'Don't mention the S-word ever again. Ever! I'm never doing one of your spells as long as I live.'

'OK, what else can I do to help?' she said sadly.

'Stake out Aleesha's house and let me know when the police and Nathan leave. I need to check the place for evidence myself. It's obvious Romeo's not looking at any other suspects apart from Brad, and I'm hoping the police might've overlooked something that leads to Nathan. If I can find proof Brad's not involved, Romeo will have to do something about it.'

'Okily dokily.' She nodded vigorously. 'You can trust me.' She looked at her watch. 'What time do you have?'

I shrugged. 'Hacker said it was half-three, why?'

Tia tapped her watch. 'We need to synchronize, Red Fox.'

I rolled my eyes.

'Come on.' Hacker tugged my arm, and we made our way out to my Toyota. 'Do you want to drive?'

'I don't think I could without crashing into something.' I tossed him my keys.

As we pulled up in the car park at Dr Spork's flat, he hurried down the stairs for his appointment with Suzy. We watched until he'd walked down the road before we got out of the car. I saw Dad's car in the car park, but he wasn't in it. Knowing Dad, he was probably dressed as a tramp or a tree doing a stakeout of Curtis's place. I phoned him to let him know he could stand down from his stakeout.

'Curtis is off the suspect list,' I told Dad.

'OK. What next, then?'

I pursed my lips, thinking. I'd discounted Steve and Jessie before, but what if one of them was involved? Both could've had access to Aleesha's keys and Nathan's tea at the studio, if Nathan's story was even true. It seemed far-fetched to me, but it wouldn't hurt just to double check. I rattled off Steve's details. 'Search his place and see what you can find. He might still be at the studio now, so hopefully his place will be empty.'

'Received and understood.' Dad hung up.

Hacker and I walked to Dr Spork's apartment. We took one glance around to make sure no one was

162

looking and pulled on some latex gloves. Hacker got out his lock-picking device and was through the flimsy lock in a no time.

We stepped inside. Hacker's gaze rested on the painting of Planet Spork.

'Wow, this is one weird guy.'

'I know.' I eyed the dirty washing pile on the sofa. 'Well, I don't think he's been doing any laundry lately. Picking up dirty T-shirts and smelly jeans, I went through everything carefully as Hacker searched the bedroom and bathroom. Luckily, his flat was small. Hopefully we would get done and dusted before he left his appointment with Suzy.

Forty-five minutes later, Hacker reappeared at my side with five packets of chocolate knickers in his hand. 'I found these, but no clothes or surfaces or anything else with traces of glitter and chocolate stains on them.'

'Me neither.' I stared at the packets of knickers, the cogs of my brain turning. 'I think the chocolate knickers are too convenient. It was plastered all over the press when Dr Spork stalked Aleesha with them, and Felicia must've got the idea from him to copy so it would look like he was at it again and get blamed.'

'He is at it again.'

'Yeah, but this time with me.' I curled up my lip.

I took the knickers out of the box and examined them. Strong nylon covered the elastic parts around the rims. You could easily strangle someone with them if you had the strength. 'As a choice of murder weapon, chocolate knickers would be pretty low on my list. There are easier ways to kill someone.' And that's when it really hit me. Brad couldn't have done this. 'Brad's trained to kill with his bare hands.

There's no way he'd strangle someone with a pair of knickers. Not when he could snap her neck in one quick move.'

'And he wouldn't leave any evidence.'

How could I have doubted Brad? I mentally kicked myself. What kind of a fiancée was I? I didn't have time to feel yet more guilt, though; I had a murderer to find.

Chapter 14

'I've got some bummer news,' Tia told me down the phone as we left Dr Spork's. 'I don't think you've got any chance of getting into Aleesha's house. The media are camped out at the gates, waiting to get a comment about Aleesha's death from Nathan. It's swarming down here. Ten-four, Red Fox?'

I rubbed my forehead, trying to get rid of the headache that now felt like a hammer drill in my head, knock, knock, knocking to get out. 'Great,' I groaned. 'We need some other kind of distraction to get them away from there. Let me have a think and call you back.'

'Roger that, Red Fox! Penelope Pitstop over and out.'

'It's *got* to be Nathan,' I said to Hacker. 'He had the opportunity and a big motive to kill her for the inheritance. And the drugged tea just doesn't sit right with me.'

'Lots of other people have got a motive, too. Or maybe it was someone we haven't even figured into the equation yet. Someone who took the opportunity to kill her so it would get blamed on the stalker sending her the death threats and knickers.'

I didn't want to admit what Hacker said might be true, because how could I investigate someone I didn't even know existed?

'How can we get the press away from Aleesha's

house and get Nathan out of the way?' I said.

'The only way you'll get the paparazzi away is if there's a bigger story elsewhere.'

'I've got an idea. Let's go back to the office.'

Half an hour later, we arrived at Hi-Tec. With no Brad or Tia, the place felt empty and very quiet. Deathly quiet. Thoughts of Brad locked up in a cell jumped into my head, and my stomach swirled with anxiety. I pictured him on death row, taking the final walk of his life down an empty corridor with stark grey walls, heading towards a bed where they'd give him a lethal injection. The doctor filled a syringe with clear liquid. He released the plunger a little, and the poison squirted out the end of the syringe. Then he looked over his shoulder and laughed maniacally. OK, so we didn't have the death penalty in the UK, but my mind was working overtime.

I shook my head to clear the chilling image. When this was over, I was so going to make it up to Brad for doubting him.

If it was over. What if he got convicted and sentenced to life imprisonment? Plenty of people had been convicted on less, and the only evidence so far pointed to Brad's hands having been in very close contact with Aleesha's neck.

'Oh, God,' I said, feeling sick, my breath coming out in ragged gasps.

'Put your head between your legs.' Hacker gently guided me to a chair and pressed on my back, pushing my head down.

'What if I never see Brad again? What if he's locked up forever?'

He rubbed my back. 'We'll get whoever the killer is. You always solve a case, and there's no way I'm

166

letting Brad get convicted of something he didn't do. He saved my life on more than one occasion. If it's the last thing I do, I'm going to save his.'

I didn't say anything because for once, I didn't know what to say.

'What's your plan?' Hacker stopped rubbing.

I shot up, and all the blood rushed to my head, making me woozy. I waited for the black and white stars behind my eyeballs to disappear before saying, 'I have to find a way to get Nathan out of the house.' I leaned forward on my desk, head in my hands.

Think, Amber!

The only thing I could come up with under short notice and a lot of stress was bringing Nathan into Hi-Tec to answer more questions about the circumstances surrounding Aleesha's death. But it was a long shot. Would he even come? Nathan was probably the murderer, so he wouldn't want to put himself under scrutiny. And he could use the excuse that since Brad had been charged with Aleesha's murder, he wouldn't want to assist the killer's colleagues in trying to set him free. Romeo would be tied up with paperwork for hours, so he wouldn't have time to give Nathan an update yet. Could I convince Nathan that the police were having second thoughts about Brad and would turn their attention towards him soon, unless he could convince everyone it wasn't an inside job and he was innocent of any involvement?

Only one way to find out.

I reached for the phone and dialled his mobile.

It rang and rang. Just as I was giving up hope he would answer, he picked up.

'Hi, Nathan, it's Amber.'

He let out an almighty sniff. 'What do you want? I don't want to be associating with someone who's tied to my sister's killer.'

'Well, that's why I'm ringing you. The police aren't convinced Brad is the real killer.' OK, an eensy weensy lie there, but it wasn't like I had any choice. 'They already suspect it's an inside job, and it won't be long before they start turning their attention to you.'

He gasped. 'Me? I would never kill her. I loved her! I just don't understand how it happened. I don't know what to do. I'm stuck in this big house all on my own, and the paparazzi won't leave me alone.' The wailing started again.

He was going pretty overboard with the fake distraught brother routine.

'Please, you have to help me,' he said breathlessly. 'I didn't have anything to do with her death. How can I convince the police not to put me away?' Humongous sniff. 'I don't want to get attacked in prison. They like boys like me, and I don't want to get hurt,' he shrieked. 'I broke my little toe once, and the pain was excruciating. Imagine what those big bullies would do to me in there!'

'I want to help you, Nathan,' I said sympathetically. I could be as good an actor as he could if I wanted. 'There is a way you can help to clear this up and get the police off your back...' I trailed off, waiting for him to take the bait.

'What? What? I'll do anything,' he said when I didn't continue.

'I'll need you to come into Hi-Tec offices and meet with my assistant, Tia. She'll go through with you everything that happened on the day Aleesha

168

was killed in minute detail, and she'll try and find some clue as to who the real killer could be.'

'Absolutely. Anything you say. As long as the police don't arrest me and take me to prison. When do you want me to come in?'

'Now would be good.'

'OK. Right away. I'm leaving now.' He paused. 'Amber?'

'Yes?'

'Promise you won't let them take me away?'

I crossed my fingers. 'I promise.' Oops, I was going to lying hell for that one.

I hung up and looked over at Hacker. 'Right, so that sorts Nathan out. Some of the paparazzi will probably follow him here, but we need to get rid of the stragglers who might hang around outside the house waiting for him to come back.' I chewed on my bottom lip, trying to think of something that would work.

My eyes met Hacker's as an idea formed. 'Brad Pitt's just arrived at Stansted Airport with Angelina Jolie,' I said.

'Have they?' He frowned.

I rolled my eyes. 'No, but if they did, the press would be down there like a shot.' Stansted Airport was only half an hour away. No way would the paparazzi want to miss that. A dead glamour girl's brother could wait if Brangelina turned up. 'So, we need to put it over all the social media that hundreds of fans are waiting for them at the airport, and their private jet's just arrived. I want you to make up fake tweets and Facebook messages and leak it to the paparazzi. Now.' I nodded towards Hacker's bank of computers and made urgent hurry up motions with my hands.

His lips curled into a grin. 'No problem.' He cracked his knuckles.

I called Tia as Hacker got to work.

'Hey, Red Fox!' she squealed down the phone.

'Tia, listen very carefully, because I don't have time for spy talk, OK?'

'Yes, Amber. Listening carefully.'

'Nathan is going to leave the house soon and come to Hi-Tec to meet with you. Follow him back here and then take him into the conference room. He's going to try to convince you that he's innocent of killing Aleesha. I want you to go through with him every single thing that happened yesterday, from the minute they got up in the morning until the minute he allegedly found her murdered. When he's gone through it once, go over it again. And again. And again. I need you to keep him here as long as you can so we can search the house. Say whatever you need to that convinces him you're trying to help him get the police off his back because they're going to start suspecting him. I'll text you when we've finished and it's OK to let him leave. Got that?'

'Affirmative.'

'Pretend that you believe he has nothing to do with Aleesha's death. Put him at ease, and just keep him talking.'

'Gotcha.'

'I'll make sure some of the underwriting staff stays in the office in case of any problems, OK?'

'Okily dokily.'

Wow, this was good. Tia was actually listening to me for once.

'Brad's life depends on you doing this right. Can I

170

trust you, Tia?'

'Absolutely. One hundred percento. I'll prove to you just what a good assistant I can be. You don't have to worry about a thing.'

I sent up a silent prayer, desperately hoping that was true. 'Great.'

'Ooh, the paparazzi are all getting in their cars and shooting off. Maybe there's a bigger story happening at the moment.'

I gave Hacker a grin and a thumbs up. Whatever he'd done had worked.

'Nathan's coming out of the drive now. I'll follow him back to the office. Gotta go!'

Next, I phoned Dad. 'I need all hands on deck. We have to search Aleesha's house before Nathan gets back.'

'Well, Steve's still at home, so I'm not doing much anyway except hanging around. Do you want me to swing by and pick up your mum to help?'

I pictured Mum rifling through Aleesha's sex toy drawer and making notes so she could try things out on Dad later. Still, an extra pair of hands would be helpful. 'We'll meet you both at your house.'

It was dark when Hacker and I pulled up on my parents' drive. Mum and Dad were dressed covertly head to toe in black. Mum wore the leather Catwoman suit I'd seen in Lace. She was even wearing black eye shadow and black lipstick. God knows where she'd got that from.

'This is so exciting!' Mum said. 'Staking out shops, following people, breaking into a house to gather evidence. It's so James Bond. And when we get back, let's all have a martini to celebrate, shaken not stirred. I've even painted my toenails black to be colour coordinated!'

When would this day ever end?

'Let me just check on Sabre quickly,' Dad said.

I followed him to the doors in the lounge and looked out over his shoulder into the garden. Sabre lay on his back, all four legs in the air, having a peaceful snooze. The neighbours' cat lay on Sabre's stomach, licking his face. Interspecies love. How cute.

'OK, let's go,' Dad said.

We all piled into Hacker's Range Rover and drove off. 'It's a go, go, go!' Mum cried out.

I turned round and raised an eyebrow at her.

'What? That's what the police always say when I've watched the *Police, Camera, Action!* chases on TV.' She paused for breath, only a slight one, mind you. 'Now I understand why you and your father are workaholics. All this catching criminals and going undercover is just fascinating.' She glanced at Dad. 'We can be a crime fighting duo from now on. Like Batman and Robin. No, Catwoman and...' She paused for another slight breath, thinking. 'Who goes with Catwoman?'

'Tom cat?' I muttered, just for something to say to take my mind off the drivel.

'Or, I know! I can buy a Wonder Woman outfit,' Mum prattled on.

I started to count to ten before I answered. I only got to six before my phoned buzzed with a text, which was quite lucky, because I might've sworn at Mum by that point. All this amateur sleuthing and spy talk with Mum and Tia was doing my head in. And anyway, being Wonder Woman was my job. I had the knickers and everything.

The text was from Tia.

'Followed Nathan to Hi-Tec with no problems. Will go and meet him. Don't worry. You can trust me. Penelope Pitstop will save the day! Xx'

I seriously hoped I could trust her. Despite her airhead exterior, she was a sharp cookie with an underlying determination and strength. I crossed my fingers she would be able to pull it off and keep Nathan there until we'd finished.

The rest of the drive passed by in silence, thank God, or I might've strangled Mum.

'So, we all know what we're looking for?' I said to everyone as we arrived at the bottom of the country lane where Aleesha's house was. 'Anything belonging to Nathan that has glitter or chocolate. Clothes, surfaces, bathrooms, or anything else that might have traces. I know there will obviously be some in Aleesha's bedroom and bathroom, but if you find any elsewhere in the house, I'm hoping it points to him. Look to see if any recent laundry has been done, too. He may have tried to wash the evidence away.'

'Message received and understood, Red Fox,' Mum said.

Hacker parked the Range Rover in a field so the vehicle wouldn't be seen from the road and strapped on a black backpack as he exited the car. 'Let's do this.'

Aleesha's house backed onto acres of farmer's fields. We crept through the dark night and approached the house from the rear.

Mum glanced up at the ten-foot wall. 'How am I going to get up there? I'm not as young and supple as I used to be.'

173

'I bet Wonder Woman wouldn't say that,' I said. 'And she must be the same age as you now.'

She nodded firmly. 'Good point.'

'I'll go over first, then throw a rope back to you.' Hacker scaled the wall like a spider, dropping down to the other side in perfect silence. A true ex-SAS professional at work.

Mum unfortunately broke the silence by whispering, 'You can be Spider-Man!'

Hacker threw the rope from his backpack over the wall. Mum grabbed it, hoisting herself to the top of the wall as Dad and I simultaneously pushed her upwards with all our strength. When she reached the top, she swung one leg over, and I heard a ripping sound from her Catwoman outfit.

'Damn. I'm going to take this suit back and a get a refund tomorrow. It's not built for actual crime fighting!' Mum swung her other leg over the wall and looked down at Hacker. 'Can you catch me?'

'Yes. But don't jump off. Ease yourself down with your arms so you're lower first, and I'll grab your waist.'

Too late. Mum launched herself off the wall, and I heard a thud as Hacker hit the deck, probably with Mum on top of him.

'Sorry. Maybe I need to lose a few pounds if I'm going to be Wonder Woman.'

'I think you broke my dose,' Hacker said in a nasally twang.

'Oops. I'm so sorry. Is it bad? Does it hurt?'

Hacker made a noise that sounded like a small grunt.

I grabbed hold of the rope and climbed up. I swung my legs over the wall and used my arms to drop down a bit before Hacker grabbed my waist and plonked me on the ground.

'See, that's how Wonder Woman does it,' I said to Mum, then stared at Hacker's nose, which was swelling rapidly. 'Are you OK?'

'I've had worse injuries than this in the line of fire.'

When Dad was over, we crept silently through the grounds of Aleesha's garden (three cheers for silence!). Hacker had already got into the security system remotely and disabled the alarm and security lights, so there was no chance of a signal notifying the police. Now we just had to find some kind of evidence that Nathan had killed her.

As Hacker made light work of the lock on the French doors in one of the downstairs rooms, I gnawed on my lip, picturing Brad sitting in that cell in a striped prison costume. I could imagine his anger at the false accusation of murder simmering away under the surface. The guilt he must feel that he could've somehow prevented her death by taking the threats more seriously. But we'd both thought Aleesha was responsible for the letters herself. How wrong could we be? And regardless of my personal feelings about her, she didn't deserve to be murdered. I worried about what Brad would do when all his anger and guilt bubbled to the surface. I wouldn't fancy being Romeo when he finally blew. A picture of me in my Fandango wedding dress at the Chapel of Love for our Vegas Elvis wedding sprang into my head. I walked down the aisle to 'Love Me Tender', laughing. Brad stood next to Elvis, looking incredibly sexy in a suit that moulded to his firm body and wearing a dangerously

175

smouldering smile. Would it ever happen now? Or would we have a prison wedding? Eeek! Conjugal visits in prison weren't high on the top of my honeymoon bucket list.

I shook my head to get visions of the prison vicar marrying us out of my brain and snapped to attention.

'This place is massive, but we need to be quick *and* thorough.' I handed out latex gloves for us all.

We entered the lounge, and Hacker shut the door behind us.

'Mum and Dad, you take the downstairs. Hacker and I can do the upstairs. And please, please don't leave anything uncovered. We can't afford to miss anything. Brad's life depends on it,' I pleaded.

'Affirmative, Red Fox,' Mum said.

We split up, Mum and Dad starting in the kitchen as Hacker and I climbed the ornate stairs that led to the top floor. I started in Nathan's bedroom, and Hacker took the room opposite. At least, I thought I was in Nathan's room. There was a huge watercolour painting of him on the wall, and a magical-looking bed, complete with a gold canopy and turrets carved onto the bedposts. Gold walls, gold cupboards, and even a golden carpet.

I got to work in the cupboards and drawers, examining all the clothes and shoes. Yes, it was Nathan's room, although his choice of wardrobe was very dodgy. I found some more leather trousers, a leather waistcoat, and even a pink fedora hat, but no signs of smeary chocolate or glitter anywhere. I rifled through the sheets, under the bed, in the en suite bathroom, and through two bins. I found all sorts of things I really didn't want to, but nothing

176

that could possibly connect him to Aleesha's death.

I let out an almighty sigh as I texted Tia to get an update on Nathan.

'Is he co-operating? Are you keeping him busy?'

'Yes. Penolop Pitstop aways ets the job don. Exting with my hand uneder the tabel.'

Well, at least that was something, but when I finally shut Nathan's bedroom door, an overwhelming sense of helplessness and anxiety pressed down in the centre of my chest. Popping my head in the bedroom Hacker was searching, I said, 'Have you found anything?'

He shook his head solemnly. 'Do,' he said, which I think meant no, but his nose had now turned huge.

Between Hacker and me, we searched every room upstairs, and a thousand years later (OK, so it was probably only about three hours, but it felt like a lifetime), we retraced our steps downstairs. The only place we'd found any glitter or chocolate was Aleesha's bedroom and bathroom, which was expected and not very helpful in proving Nathan's involvement.

We found Mum in the utility room and Dad in the downstairs toilet just off it. Mum was searching the laundry basket as Dad examined the plughole in the sink with a torch.

'Did you find anything that could help?' I asked Dad, more pleading than a question.

'I'm afraid not.'

'Looks like he hasn't done any washing since last night,' Mum said. 'The machine is dry, and there's a pile of laundry left. I've just gone through it all, but there are no traces of glitter or chocolate.'

My shoulders slumped. Unless I could come up

with something, Brad was completely screwed.

I texted Tia and told her to let Nathan go in ten minutes. We all left the house, making our way back over the fields. My legs felt rubbery with fatigue, and my heartbeat fluttered erratically against my ribs. I was sure Nathan had killed her. I suppose he could've destroyed the evidence, but did he have the time or opportunity? The police were there all morning and would've seen him trying to burn or bury evidence on the grounds, the paparazzi were camped out on the driveway, and Tia had followed him when he left the house, so he couldn't have done anything then, either. We found no traces of glitter in any of the pipes or traps from the showers or sinks, apart from Aleesha's. Even if Nathan had worn gloves to strangle her, he would've surely washed his hands afterwards if he'd done the dirty deed. Unless he was clever enough to wash his hands in Aleesha's bathroom. But the glitter would've still got onto some part of his skin or clothes, and yet there were no traces of transfer anywhere. And strangling someone, looking into their eyes as the life flowed out of them, took a hardened kind of killer. Somehow, Nathan didn't seem like the kind of guy to pull off a perfect murder. He was too high strung and drama queenish. I had to admit I'd been wrong about him. He must've been telling the truth. Which left me where?

'So, if it wasn't Nathan, it had to be someone else who knew the alarm code and got into the house with no sign of forced entry,' I said as we drove back down the country lane. 'And someone who had access to Nathan's tea.'

And then my brain pinged into idea mode. Nathan

said Aleesha was always leaving her keys and phone everywhere on set. Her keys weren't missing, so someone must've taken a copy. Then I thought about the alarm code. They had to keep changing it whenever Aleesha dumped another guy, just in case. We had so many pin numbers and passwords for things these days, I couldn't keep up or remember them all. What if Aleesha had to change her alarm code so often that she couldn't remember it anymore and wrote it down, leaving the note in her bag with her keys? Or what if Aleesha stored the code in her phone under a fake number? That meant anyone at the studio or at a photo shoot could've got hold of it. But Nathan also said he'd already had his daily afternoon cup of nettle tea while Aleesha was filming *Real Women*, so he wouldn't have taken the tea into the *Playboy* shoot. Which meant the killer had to be someone with access to the studio kitchen, where Nathan left his tea for everyone to help themselves, and the *Real Women* set, where someone could copy Aleesha's keys and alarm code. The code hadn't been changed for two weeks because Steve and the guy Aleesha dumped him for, Alfonso, had never been to the house and couldn't have seen it. Jessie was sacked two weeks ago. She stormed off after being fired and finding out about their affair, so she could've got the alarm code and copied the keys before she left. She'd also threatened to kill Aleesha. Were those threats in the heat of anger, or did she really act on them? Plus, Jessie was known on set. I bet it wouldn't have been hard for her to slip into the studio on the day Aleesha died, spike Nathan's tealeaves, and then leave. Had my empathy for Jessie made me miss something I should've seen all along? Was she just an amazing actress who completely fooled me?

On the other hand, maybe Steve wasn't as embarrassed about being manipulated by Aleesha as he seemed. Maybe he was angry with Aleesha instead, blaming her for losing Jessie. Angry enough to kill?

Eeny, meeny, miny, mo.

Or maybe Steve and Jessie were in it together. A Bonnie and Clyde murder team. Or was it someone else who worked at the studio? Someone who held a secret grudge against Aleesha? What about Tania Tate, the *Real Women* co-host? She said she got on well with Aleesha and liked her, but was that just a lie? Was she harbouring a secret hatred of her? Had Aleesha stabbed her in the back, too, as she'd done to so many others?

I mentally banged my head on the dashboard, feeling so helpless as my mind sifted through all the possibilities. There were just too many maybes and not enough hard facts to go on.

Hacker and I dropped Mum and Dad off at home and drove back to my car in the Hi-Tec car park as I mulled everything over.

'I remember watching the live show of *Children in Need* the night Aleesha was killed, and Tania Tate was hosting it,' I said. 'Can you get hold of a recording of it and find out the exact time Tania was at the studio until? Maybe I can rule her out, too, if she was at the studio all night. I think it was supposed to be live from eight p.m. to eight a.m.'

'Will do. It may take me a while, but I'll stay up all night if I have to.' He parked up, turned off the engine, and gave my shoulder a squeeze.

'Thanks.' I gave him a pained smile.

Time was running out, and it was too late to do anything else tonight. Tomorrow I had to find the real killer.

Chapter 15

It was one a.m. when I finally crawled into bed, exhausted and defeated. Marmalade snuggled up beside me, sensing something was wrong.

'I'm not talking to you anymore. You told me Brad slept with Aleesha, and I don't think he did.' I scratched him behind the ear.

He eyed me nonchalantly, waiting for me to carry on talking. Even Marmalade knew I couldn't keep up the silent treatment for long. My mouth had a mind of its own and loved to blab.

He blinked his huge green eyes at me and, of course, I couldn't stop myself.

'OK, maybe you didn't actually say "yes" before. Perhaps "me meow" means maybe. Is that it? Meow once for "yes" and twice for "no".' I gave him a stern look.

'Meow.'

Right. I got it now. As long as we were clear on this. So, the only good thing to happen all day was that Marmalade had increased his vocabulary from just 'yes' and 'no' to 'maybe' as well.

'So who's the killer?' I was rapidly running out of suspects, and so far, all my instincts on this case had been completely wrong. I seriously doubted my ability to find the truth before it was too late.

Marmalade blinked at me and rolled onto his back, letting me stroke his soft belly.

'Steve?' I asked hopefully.

Purr.

'Or Jessie?'

Louder purr.

'Tania?'

Marmalade sneezed.

I sighed at him. 'What does that mean? Why can't you talk sense anymore? Are you missing Brad? Is that it?'

'Meow.'

'Me, too, boy. Me, too.' Turning over onto my side, I stared at Brad's empty spot on the bed. I touched the cold sheets, wondering if he'd ever be in this bed with me again. I grabbed his pillow and hugged it tight, inhaling the traces of his aftershave and musky, manly smell like it was a drug.

The next morning I woke up in the same position, wrapped around Brad's pillow. Marmalade was lying on my head. No wonder I kept waking up with headaches. It was nothing to do with the wine after all.

I forced myself to eat a slice of toast before I wasted away, but the bread felt like sandpaper in my mouth, and it took all the effort I had to swallow each piece. I gave Marmalade a kiss on the head and went upstairs to grab a suit, shirt, and tie for Brad to wear in court.

Court! Yikes. They wanted to hold him in custody with no bail until the trial.

No, Amber. There won't be a trial. You'll catch the killer. You will.

As I was putting Brad's clothes in a suit carrier, Hacker phoned.

'Yo,' I said. 'How's your nose?'

'It's a bit sore, but I'll live.'

'Did you watch the *Children in Need* show?'

'Yep. Tania was on live TV from eight p.m. until eight a.m. In between presenting, there were obviously segments, bands, and sketches, but the longest was only thirty minutes. There's no way she would've had time to leave the studio, get to Aleesha's house and kill her, then back again. Tania's definitely off the suspect list.'

'OK, thanks, Hacker. I'm going to see Brad now. Then I'll stake out Jessie's place. Hopefully, I can get inside while she's out somewhere and take a look around. I'll get Dad to cover Steve's. They're the only two possible suspects left on my list. And if it isn't either of them, Brad's in deep shit.'

'Good luck. And tell Brad we're doing all we can. Yo.'

I hung up and motored towards Hertford Police station, arriving at eight a.m. on the dot. As I climbed up the steps of the building where I used to work for seventeen years, I wondered how things could go so badly wrong in such a short space of time. Brad and I were jinxed. Our whole relationship had been complicated from the start. Maybe we just weren't supposed to be together. Maybe this was really a sign. I mean, having your fiancé banged up for murder a few days before the wedding couldn't possibly be a good sign, could it?

'Hi, Amber, how's things?' the duty officer on the front desk, who I'd known for years, said to me.

I pulled a face. 'Not good.'

'I suppose you're here to see Brad?' he asked sheepishly, as if it was his fault.

'Yes. Can you tell the custody sergeant I'm here,

please?'

He disappeared behind the desk. His footsteps squeaked on the lino floor up the corridor to where the cells were located. Cells I'd put many prisoners into during my time there.

I stood at the desk and tapped my foot as an elderly woman shuffled to the counter in her slippers. She wore a thick tweed coat and curlers in her bluish-tinted hair.

'I want to see my son who's been arrested,' she said to the duty officer who'd reappeared behind the desk.

The door behind me that led into the building opened and dragged my attention away from the old lady. A bubbly woman with fiery red hair practically shot out the door towards me. Carole Blake, the coroner's officer and a good friend, squished me in a big hug.

'I heard what happened. God, I'm so sorry.' She pulled back.

'He didn't do it, Carole. But I've just got to find some way of proving it.'

She nodded sympathetically. 'You don't think it's because Brad stole you from Romeo, do you? You know, maybe Romeo's got it in for him now and he's trying to stop the wedding. '

I'd thought about that. A lot. But Romeo was a good guy and a good police officer. I think he genuinely believed Brad had killed Aleesha.

'No one can steal someone who doesn't want to be stolen,' I said. It wasn't as if I was a possession, like a car or favourite keepsake. Maybe Romeo did still have strong feelings for me, but I didn't think he'd seriously get Brad put away for murder to prevent us being together.

Carole rubbed my arm. 'Well, I'm sure you'll find out who did it, Amber. Listen, I have to shoot off. I've got another suspicious death scene to go to. Good luck.' She gave me one last hug and left through the front entrance.

I tapped my foot and stared at the wanted posters on the information board, wondering if Brad and I could make a run for it. Could I spring him from the cells, and we could hide out somewhere until I found the real killer? I let out a deflated sigh. Nope. It wouldn't do any good.

The elderly woman's voice grew louder behind me as she demanded to see her son, who was apparently in one of the cells.

'You have no right to keep him locked up in one of those padded cells!' the woman shrieked at the officer.

'It's not a padded cell, ma'am.'

'He needs his memory foam mattress, not a hard trolley to sleep on.' The woman ran a shaky hand through her hair. 'How can you keep him in there with the common criminals?'

'I'm afraid he's been charged with breach of the peace, ma'am. He swore at an officer.'

'How could he swear at an officer?' the old woman cried. 'He's deaf, and he can't speak, either!'

'He signed the swear word, ma'am.'

'What do you mean?' The elderly woman frowned.

'He swore at the officer in sign language.'

'How did the police officer even understand sign language?' the woman asked skeptically. 'I still haven't mastered it yet, and I've been trying to learn it for twenty years.'

186

'Well, everyone knows the "V" sign, ma'am.'

At that moment, Sergeant Napier, who I'd worked with before, opened the door behind me, breaking into my thoughts about me wanting to use the 'V' sign on a certain police officer.

'Hi, Amber,' Sergeant Napier said solemnly. 'I hear you want to see Brad.'

My throat squeezed closed with emotion, and the words stuck in my throat, so I just nodded.

'Come on, then. I'll give you ten minutes.'

I followed him down the hall to the cells. Felicia's name was marked on a board outside the cell next to Brad's. She would probably be up in court this morning for the threatening letters.

Sergeant Napier opened a little hatch on the door of Brad's cell and looked in. 'Visitor for you,' he said to Brad before unlocking the heavy steel door.

I walked in. Brad sat on a thin metal bed at one end of the small cell, wearing a police issue jumpsuit. Sergeant Napier shut the door with a loud clang and locked it behind him, leaving the hatch open.

Brad stood up, and I dumped the carry case on the bed and fell into his arms. Resting my head against his shoulder, I felt myself melt into his warm body. I breathed in his rugged, musky scent, the traces of his aftershave still lingering on him. I slid one hand up the taut muscles along his back and one hand around his neck, pulling him to me in an urgent kiss. What if I never felt his lips on mine again, or any other part of my body, for that matter? What if we didn't get to grow old together like we were supposed to?

'How are you?' I leaned back, studying his face, as if trying to commit it to memory in case I hardly

187

ever got to see him again.

'I've been captured by terrorists and had tortured interrogations. This is a piece of cake.' The edges of his lips curved into a slight grin, but even if it was true, I knew he was only saying it for my benefit. My heart swelled with love. Here he was, stuck in a crappy cell, accused of murder, and he was trying to put me at ease and stop me going out of mind with worry.

'God, I've missed you.' He pulled me in for another full lip-lock, which would've got my nipples springing to attention if we weren't in a police cell. Not very conducive to arousal, let me tell you.

I pressed my flat palm to his chest and pushed him to sit on the bed. Sitting next to him and holding his hand, I told him what I'd found out so far, which was bugger all.

'So it looks like the only possible suspects we have left are Jessie and Steve,' I said.

'Or someone we don't know about yet.'

'That's also possible, which could narrow it down to thousands, with the amount of people she's pissed off over the years.'

'But it had to be someone at the set of *Real Women*,' Brad said. 'Someone with access to Aleesha's keys who also had access to Nathan's tea and knew his tea-drinking habits. Since he only has one cup in the afternoon and one before bedtime, they would've had to make sure they drugged the tea *after* he'd had his afternoon cuppa on set for their plan to work.' Brad tucked a crazy curl away from my face. He was trying to be calm about it, but a muscle in his jaw throbbed with tension. 'The wedding's not looking good, Foxy.'

Tears pricked at my eyes. It was no use; I couldn't contain them any longer.

'Hey, don't cry.' He wiped away a tear snaking down my cheek, and I leaned into his hand. He slid his other arm around me, pulling me tight.

'What time are you up in front of the magistrate this morning?' I rested my head on his shoulder, wishing I could stay there forever.

'Ten a.m. It looks like they'll keep me in custody with no bail until the trial.'

'That's not going to happen.' I lifted my head up and stared into his steely eyes, eyes that held a hint of despair and worry. 'I'll find out who did this, even if it kills me.'

Sergeant Napier appeared and shouted through the hatch, 'Your time's up, I'm afraid.'

As he unlocked the door, I gave Brad one last kiss on the lips and left him with a determined smile. I was so going to prove Romeo wrong.

Exiting the police station, I saw Dr Spork heading my way with a pink-wrapped package in his hand.

Great. Just what I need.

I stopped on the steps, hands on hip, glaring at him as he came towards me. I was definitely not in the mood for any erotomania today. Dr Spork stopped a few steps in front of me. His gaze darted round, not wanting to meet mine.

'I don't want any knickers.' I'd seen enough of the bloody things to last me a lifetime by now. 'The Sporkites aren't telling you that I love you. And we're not supposed to be together. OK? Got that?'

He still wouldn't look at me as he fiddled with the pink package. 'Er…these aren't for you.'

I breathed a sigh of relief. 'Who are they for,

then?'

'Felicia Seabright.' He stared at the ground. 'I heard what she did, and I think the Sporkites are telling me that she's the one for me. We've got so much in common, you see.' He finally met my gaze. 'I'm sorry to disappoint you. I know you wanted to marry me and be my Sporkite bride, but...I'm afraid I'm going to have to dump you. I'm in love with Felica.'

I did a mental fist pump in the air. *Yes!*

'Well, I think you totally deserve each other, and I'm sure you'll be very happy together.'

'So...you're not mad at me?'

'*Moi?*' I pointed a finger at myself. It was the only spot of good news I'd had all day. 'Not at all.' I jerked my head back towards the police station. 'You'd better visit her before she goes to court.'

He nodded, and his ponytail fell out of its scrunchie. 'Yes. OK, no hard feelings, then?'

'Absolutely.' I walked down the rest of the steps, thinking that Suzy seriously needed to go back to med school and retake psychiatry. Whatever she was doing wasn't working.

Chapter 16

By nine-fifteen, Dad was staking out Steve's house. *Real Women* aired live at lunchtime, so Steve would be going to the studio soon. Dad could get in there and have a good rummage around while he was out. Mum had been out early that morning and bought a James Bond boxed set of DVDs to watch and get tips from. I seriously hoped I never had to use her or Tia on another case.

I'd been so sure before that Steve or Jessie had nothing to do with this, but my judgement had been seriously flawed lately. After all, I'd thought Brad might've been having a fling with Aleesha and could've killed her, and there's no way he would've done either of those things. He loved me. I knew that, and I was an idiot to doubt it even for a second. I'd got everything so wrong by suspecting Aleesha of sending the letters for publicity that I'd overlooked a killer. And Brad now had to live with the fact that he hadn't protected her properly, and she'd paid a deadly price.

I was parked up a little way down the road from Jessie Hinds's house, drinking a mochaccino and eating one of the healthy birdseed bars Hacker and Brad usually ate. I was off chocolate for life, and since my clothes were already getting loose after I'd lost my appetite, I needed some body fuel. My wedding dress would look crap if it was all hangy and rumply and didn't fit my body. And I was determined that I was bloody well wearing that dress. In Vegas. With Brad. In four days. Actually, the bar wasn't that bad. It was kind of nice and...crunchy. Who knew health food could taste OK? Not that it would cure me of my junk food addiction. It was just temporary. As soon as Brad was out of custody, I'd be overdosing on burgers, chips, and sugary cinnamon doughnuts. It would be my reward for capturing the real killer. So would lots of sex with Brad, minus the death by chocolate fantasy, though.

I changed position in my seat and yawned, glancing at the dashboard clock. Ten a.m. Brad would be at court. I chewed on a fingernail, wondering what was happening. I wanted to be there to give him some moral support, but clearing his name was more important.

By eleven-thirty I was edgy and busting for a wee. I pressed my thighs together.

Oops, bad idea! It made my bladder want to burst. I eyed the empty Starbucks coffee cup. Would anyone notice if I...

All thoughts of my bladder disappeared as Jessie backed out of her driveway in her Audi convertible. I ducked down until she drove past.

Was she the killer? Hopefully, I'd soon find out.

I glanced up and down the street. No one was around. Good. I grabbed the stun gun from my rucksack and stuffed it in the side pocket of my combats. Then I took my handcuffs and shoved them in my back pocket. I made my way up her drive calmly, trying to look innocent, like I wasn't just about to break and enter for what felt like the thousandth time this week. I was getting good at this. If I ever felt like giving up insurance investigating, I could become a cat burglar.

I pulled Hacker's lock-picking tool out of the pocket of my combats and followed a gravel path to the side gate. Pressing down the latch sounded loud in the silence. I checked around again to see if anyone was about, but big bushes obscured me from view of the road. The only other noise was my pulse pumping hard in my ears.

I slipped through the gate and shut it behind me, making my way along the side of the building. There was a small window with privacy glass above me. Bathroom or toilet. It looked too small to crawl through, so I carried on round the corner of the house, coming to a single double-glazed door that led to a utility room.

Lock-picking device to the rescue. After watching Brad and Hacker do it so many times, it was easy. Within a minute, I was inside the lemon-painted room. Underneath a window, there was a sink unit with a washing machine and dryer underneath. I opened the door to each and looked inside.

Empty of washing.

A clothes airer was folded against the back wall with nothing on it, and I found nothing of interest in the cupboards along one wall. No traces of glitter in the sink.

The door squeaked open as I made my way through into the kitchen. My bladder shouted at me, reminding me it needed some serious attention. Jessie wouldn't notice if I had a quick wee while I was here.

I padded through the kitchen, past an under stairs

cupboard on one side and the lounge on the other, and looked for a downstairs toilet. Surprisingly, there wasn't one, so I ran up the stairs. Straight in front of me was the bathroom. Hurrah! I yanked down my combats, and my bladder gave a sigh of relief. I glanced around the room as I did my business. Modern sink with a chrome mixer tap and a blue liquid soap dispenser on top. A distressed wood-framed mirror above that. Under sink cupboard. The bath had a shower screen attached, and a loofah hung from the taps. Bottles of shampoo and...hang on a sec.

My gaze cut back to the sink. Right at the bottom edge, facing the toilet, was something glittery. I shot off the loo, wiped, and pulled up my combats. I crouched down to stare at it.

Yep, there is was. A tiny smudge of silver glitter, and if I hadn't been sitting on the toilet, I probably never would've spotted it. Yay, three cheers for bladders!

I pulled my phone out of my pocket and dialled Romeo, wanting to get him and the crime scene team up here to analyze it before Jessie noticed the incriminating evidence and cleaned it off.

The phone rang persistently in my ear.

Come on. Pick up!

It went to voicemail.

Damn! Was he still in court with his phone turned off?

'Romeo, it's me. I've just found some smudges of glitter in Jessie's bathroom. You need to get up here quick with SOCO and examine it. Jessie's the killer, NOT Brad.' I left a breathless message and hung up, wondering what other evidence she'd left behind.

I'd seriously underestimated Jessie. What was it they said about a woman scorned?

Hurrying out of the bathroom, I made my way down the hallway. There were three closed doors. I opened the first one and stuck my head in. It was a bedroom turned into a home gym. Lots of exercise equipment that looked very tortuous to me, but no sign of any other evidence. The next room was Jessie's bedroom. I opened the door, and a gasp escaped from my lips.

The room was painted in black and red. A red lampshade with a red-coloured bulb hung from the centre of the room. The blinds were black and so were the wardrobes. Two red sets of drawers sat either side of the bed, and a black dressing table in the corner of the room. But the colour scheme wasn't the gaspable offence. The weird thing was the various assortments of chains, whips, and paddles hanging on wall hooks above the bed.

I rifled through her wardrobes, looking for any glitter or chocolate stains on her clothes. Unfortunately, I didn't find any. What I did find was lots of tight leather outfits and bondage suits, a couple of leather masks with holes cut out for the eyes and mouth, thigh high leather boots, and more assorted whips and chains.

So, not only was Jessie a murderer, she was also a dominatrix. Wow. She'd never struck me as the type when I first met her. I thought she was too innocent to be a kinky dominatrix. Then again, I didn't think she was a murderer, either. How wrong could I have been about her?

I turned away from the cupboard and spied a laundry bin in the corner of the room. I was seriously sick of going through people's dirty underwear this week. God knows what icky things I'd find in Jessie's if the rest of the room were anything to go by. Now I knew what the officials at airport customs felt like as they rummaged around in people's suitcases. I dreaded to think what items they were exposed to. I was so making sure I washed my dirty underwear before I came back from Vegas, just in case.

As I took the lid off the laundry basket, my phone rang.

'Hey, Amber, I got your message,' Romeo said. 'Do I even want to know what you're doing inside Jessie's house?'

'Look, it's not my fault I had to do a spot of breaking and entering. You were so determined to pin this on Brad, I had to look for evidence myself,' I said defensively.

I heard a sigh down the phone. 'Have you found anything else, apart from the smudges of glitter?'

'Lots of kinky sex stuff, but I'm still looking for more evidence of the murder.'

The silence down the line sounded really loud to my ears before he said, 'How do I know you haven't planted evidence at Jessie's house to get Brad off the hook?'

Anger simmered in the pit of my stomach, threatening to explode tsunami style. 'Because you know me, Romeo. How long did we work together? How long did we have a relationship together? You know I wouldn't do that.'

'Not even to save Brad? Don't forget it was you who investigated the David Leonard murder and conveniently didn't find any evidence that Brad killed him.'

'That's because there was no evidence!' I shrieked.

'Yes, but you knew it was him.'

Maybe I did, but it wouldn't do Brad any good at all if I admitted that little snippet. Plus, David Leonard was a serial killer, and the world was better off without him. 'You know as well as I do that if Brad killed Aleesha, he wouldn't have left any trace.'

'Like when he killed David Leonard or Vinnie Dawson, you mean?'

I sighed. 'Anyway, if you remember, I didn't go into Aleesha's bedroom, and I never touched her body before it was taken away by the coroner, so how could I get any of the glitter or chocolate from her skin and suddenly plant it here?' My temperature shot up with fury, but my blood ran cold. What if he didn't believe me? What if Jessie got away with it and Brad got sent to prison for life? 'Am I talking Spork language here? What part of "evidence" don't you understand?'

He mulled that over for a moment.

'Look, this is getting us nowhere. We can argue the finer points of David's murder another day,' I said. 'But right now you need to get over here and get this evidence.' I rummaged through Jessie's laundry basket as I was talking, to try to distract me from exploding with annoyance. Dresses, knickers, bras, more leather outfits, and a burgundy long-sleeved top with...

'Are you still there?' Romeo asked.

I picked up the top and examined the cuffs. 'Romeo, I've just found one of Jessie's tops in her laundry basket with more glitter and brown stains on it. Just get over here, will you?' My voice shot up a few decibels.

'OK.'

I stared up at the ceiling, exhaling a sigh of relief. *Finally!*

'Get out of the house and meet me outside,' he said. 'I'll grab SOCO and see you there soon.'

'OK.' I hung up and put the top back where I'd found it in the laundry basket. Giving the room one quick final glance, something on top of the bedside drawer caught my eye.

A gold bracelet with gold charms of the Eiffel Tower and a camera on it.

I crossed the room in three quick strides and stared at the bracelet. The last time I'd seen it, it had been hanging off Aleesha's wrist. The charms were unusual and probably had personal meaning to the owner. What were the chances of two people having exactly the same bracelet as this? Even if Jessie could somehow explain the glitter and chocolate stains, which seemed very unlikely, how could she possibly explain getting this bracelet from a dead woman?

I was so engrossed in my thoughts that I didn't hear anyone creeping up behind me.

One minute I was thinking about the bracelet, and the next, pain seared through the back of my head. I stumbled forwards into the bedside drawers, and my head cracked on the corner of it. Then the room submerged into blackness.

Chapter 17

When I came round, I had two thoughts. One, my head was so painful it felt like it was being squished in a vice. And two, I was lying on the floor between the bed and the overturned bedside drawers with something squeezing my throat and a heavy weight on my back.

My eyelids flew open. I brought my hands up to my throat, desperately clutching at the thing round my neck and trying to pull it away before I strangled to death. My head arched back with the pressure as someone pulled tighter and tighter. I saw black and white stars behind my eyeballs.

My life flashed before me. I thought about all the stupid things I'd wasted time worrying about over the years. If I ever got out of this alive, I was going to ditch the neurotic and insecure side and be happy with what I had.

'No one will ever find you,' Jessie screeched manically as she straddled my back, her weight pressing me into the floor.

She was strong, too. It looked like she'd had a lot of practice, judging by the gym equipment and the dominatrix paraphernalia. I vowed if I made it through this, I would stop eating junk and exercise regularly. The only exercise I currently did consisted of drinking games and a healthy sex life.

I fought to slide my fingers under the material so I

could make a gap between my neck and whatever she was using, and discovered it was a bra.

Omigod. I was going to die. I could imagine what my death certificate would say. 'Death by D Cups.'

The breath left my body. My face flushed with heat. My head pounded as the circulation got cut off.

Do something, quick!

My police training kicked into gear then, and an adrenaline surge shot through me. I stretched my right arm up along the floor, and pressed the palm of my left hand into the floor, elbow up and bent. Then I rolled onto my right side with all the strength I could muster. The movement was enough for me to dislodge Jessie off my back. She toppled to the side, and I twisted round so I was lying on my back. I kicked her in the side, my boots connecting with her hip.

'Ow!' She landed on her side in an awkward position.

I frantically looked round the room for something to use as a weapon. When I flew into the drawers, they'd overturned and spilled their contents onto the carpet.

I spied a heavy-duty black rubber dildo, grabbed it, and hit her over the head with it before I had time to worry about what kind of contamination I'd get.

'Bitch!' She clutched her head and rolled around on the floor. I hit her again in the face, just for good measure, and it smashed into her nose.

Jessie howled.

I reached for my handcuffs, which had fallen out of my pocket when she knocked me over, and wrestled with her. I tried to turn her onto her stomach so I could cuff her hands behind her back.

She punched me in the face.

The force sent me toppling backwards, and I landed with a hard thud right on my coccyx, the handcuffs flying onto the floor.

Argh! Flashes of hot white pain shot up my spine. I sat in a crumpled heap on the carpet, dazed for a few seconds.

She grabbed the dildo and smacked me over the head with it. Now my death certificate would read, 'Death by Dildo'! This was so wrong. I couldn't die at the hands of a sex-toy-wielding lunatic. It wasn't supposed to happen like this. When I did eventually snuff it, I would be old and wrinkly, wearing slippers, drinking cocoa, and smothering myself in cold cream and a hairnet before I went to bed. And I'd be with Brad, who was also old and wrinkly, minus the hairnet and cream.

Jessie whacked me over the head again. God knows what the dildo was made of, but it was bloody hard. My hands flew protectively to my head as the room whirled around me and my vision went funny. That gave Jessie all the time she needed to spring towards me, hands outstretched as if she was going in for a second strangulation.

She knocked me onto my back, and she was on top of me again, hands round my throat as she straddled me. I turned my head to the side, groping on the floor for another weapon. Then I remembered the stun gun in my pocket.

I reached down to the side pocket of my combats and manoeuvred the stun gun out. This was all I needed. One blast of this, and she'd be in night-night land. I held the stun gun on the flimsy material of her shirt just underneath her ribs and pressed the button.

Nothing happened.

She didn't jerk. Her eyes didn't roll back in her head. She didn't pass out from the high voltage. She didn't even twitch.

I pressed again as Jessie's fingernails dug into my skin, making me gasp for breath.

Nothing.

Oh, fuckity fuck!

I dropped the stun gun, and my fingertips connected with something else on the floor. Something almost out of reach.

Jessie's hands locked round my throat, squeezing.

I tried to grab what I could feel. It was a canister of some kind. Maybe hairspray.

The air slipped from my lungs, and my throat burned with pain. My fingertips scrambled for the can, but the more I tried to grab it, the further it rolled out of reach.

Jessie dug her fingers into my throat harder. I teetered on the edge of darkness as she cut off my oxygen supply.

Finally, I stretched my arm out with all my might and got a good grip on the can. Grabbing it, I placed my finger on the nozzle and sprayed what was actually 'Tingling Pleasure Lubrication Gel' in her eyes.

'Argh!' Jessie screamed, her hands flying to her eyes. 'You've blinded me! It's burning.'

I gulped in huge breaths of air as she rolled off me and scrambled to her feet. She tried to run out of the room, no doubt to douse her eyes with water.

I picked up my handcuffs and launched myself towards her. I rugby-tackled her to the floor as she blindly stumbled towards the bedroom door. I dug my knees in her back and pressed down on her with all my weight, trying to get hold of her wrists.

She writhed underneath me. 'You've made me blind! I'm going to kill you.'

'Not if I kill you first,' I hissed through uneven breaths, cuffing her hands behind her back.

She thrashed around beneath me. Even handcuffed, Jessie was obviously used to dishing out some nasty punishment in her dominatrix sideline, and I wasn't taking any risks. Through my wobbly vision, I spied a hardback book that had fallen out of the drawer and whacked her hard over the head with *Dominatrices through the Ages*.

Her body went slack, and she was finally still, unconscious.

I climbed off her, collapsing onto the floor and leaning back against the bed as I gulped in huge gasps of breath. My head was killing me from the whacks I'd taken with the dildo and smacking it on the drawers. Who knew a dildo could be a lethal weapon? My throat was on fire. I clutched my head in my hands, willing the throbbing pain to stop and moaning to myself.

Somewhere in the distance, I heard a door smash open downstairs and Romeo's voice calling out to me. 'Amber! Are you OK?'

I tried to call out, 'I'm here,' but it came out as, 'Flah!'

Flah? What did that mean?

Ouch. Stop thinking. It hurts to think.

Heavy footsteps ran up the stairs. The bedroom door opened. Romeo rushed in.

He took one glance at Jessie on the floor and

crouched down to me, hands on my shoulders, looking into my eyes.

Except I didn't know which Romeo to look at. Three Romeos swam before my eyes.

All three faces peered closer to mine.

'Are you OK, Amber?'

'Clappity flump flapper.'

'What?' The first Romeo said, or maybe it was the second one.

'Iffing pumple scoop.'

The third Romeo pulled something out of his pocket that I couldn't focus on.

And for the second time that day, I passed out.

Chapter 18

I heard a beeping sound as I drifted in and out of consciousness. I was sure the beeping was talking to me, but I couldn't make out what it was saying. Or maybe my muzzy brain imagined it.

My head felt all light and floaty, but at the same time, my body felt heavy. Like I was pinned down and something was crushing me.

Voices said things like 'vital signs', 'severe concussion', 'stable'.

Was I in a stable?

I tried to move my fingers, but nothing happened. I didn't want to die in a stable. It would smell of horse poo. If I was going to die, I wanted it to be with Brad.

Something touched my hand and squeezed it.

'Amber? Are you awake?' It was Romeo's voice.

You know those dreams where you're screaming but nothing's coming out? It was like that. I tried to talk but nothing happened, and the beeping sound faded into oblivion again.

The next time I can remember anything was when I was aware of a feather stroking my face. It felt good. Soft and, well, feathery. I turned my cheek towards the sensation.

Maybe this was it. Maybe I was dying, and angel wing feathers were stroking me. They were coming to take me away somewhere peaceful and happy.

205

Somewhere you could eat cake all day long and never put weight on.

'Mmm,' my croaky voice mumbled.

'Amber?' Brad's voice said urgently.

My eyelids fluttered open. Everything seemed hazy around the edges, like I had a severe case of myopia and needed double-barrel glasses. The room slipped in and out of focus, my lids like lead. Things moved in front of my eyes. I still had a burning in my throat and crushing pain in my head. My body felt bone-numbingly tired, like I'd been whizzing through an industrial food processor for weeks.

'You're OK,' Brad said. 'You're safe.'

A weight next to me on the bed. A hand squeezed mine.

'Talk to me,' Brad said.

I turned my head towards him, the room slowly coming into focus.

He rested his fingertips on my cheek. 'Can you see me? It's Brad.'

I lifted a heavy arm and touched his hand. 'Brad? Am I dead? Did the angels get me? Is there junk food in heaven?'

He gave a slight laugh of relief. 'No. You're very much alive. Thank God.'

'My head hurts,' I croaked.

'I'm not surprised. You took a good whack to it.'

'My throat hurts, too. And...' My whole body started aching then as my consciousness returned bit by bit. 'My ribs and my back.'

Slowly, it all started coming back to me. Finding the evidence in Jessie's house. The fight with her. Slipping into a pool of darkness.

'You've been out of it for almost twenty-four

hours. Your mum and dad were here earlier, but they just left to grab some sleep.'

'It was Jessie,' I croaked. It felt like I'd swallowed a cheese grater. 'She nearly strangled me with a bra.'

He brushed his lips against my ear. 'I know. I'm so glad you're safe.'

I thought about how close I'd come to losing Brad and being killed again. Tears stung my eyes. 'I think we're jinxed. Maybe we shouldn't get married. Maybe something bad will happen if we do.'

His eyes crinkled at the corners as his lips curled in a loving smile. 'We are *definitely* getting married.' He kissed me softly on the lips before pulling back abruptly. 'But I think we'll need to postpone the Vegas wedding. The flight is in three days, and I don't want to risk your health. How are you feeling?'

I didn't know which bits hurt more. 'Sore, but I'm alive, which I guess is the main thing.'

'The doctor said you had a severe concussion, but you should be OK with lots of rest. I'm going to spoil you rotten.' He winked.

A grin snaked up the corners of my lips. 'Ooh, sounds nice.' My eyelids grew heavy, and I closed my eyes.

'Are you OK?' Brad's voice rose with urgency.

'Uh-huh. I will be,' I said, eyes still closed. 'When did they let you out?'

'Last night. The police lab is still analyzing the glitter and chocolate stains from Jessie's house, but they're sure it's going to be a match.'

'I'm surprised they let you out, then. Romeo seemed pretty hell bent on keeping you inside.'

'They found the bracelet Aleesha was wearing the

night she died at Jessie's house, so they knew only the killer could've had access to it. The bracelet was actually Jessie's. Jessie had left it at Steve's house, and Aleesha stole it for a keepsake after she'd slept with him. Kind of like a notch on the bedpost. When Jessie was confronted with the evidence you found, she broke down and confessed.'

'And she used the chocolate knickers stalker as a cover.'

'Yes. Apparently, when you spoke to Jessie the first time and told her about the threats Aleesha was getting, Jessie thought she could get away with killing her and blaming it on the stalker.'

'So she planted the sleeping drugs in Nathan's tea, but how could she know that both of you would drink it on that night?'

'It was just luck on her part. In fact, she said she didn't even know I was staying at the house. Jessie knew when both Aleesha and Nathan would be on the set of *Real Women*. She also knew Nathan always drank a cup of the herbal tea while Aleesha was filming the show, and one before bedtime. So she slipped into the studio when they were on air, on the premise of seeing Steve, and put the ground-up drugs in Nathan's stash of tea after he'd had his lunchtime cup. All she had to do was wait until he drank it that night, and he'd be out like a light. Then she could sneak in and kill Aleesha. It was just unlucky that I drank it, too and got drugged in the process. Jessie said when she broke in and saw me unconscious at the kitchen table with an empty tea cup, she thought I was Aleesha's new boyfriend. She thought she'd try and frame me in the process by putting the glitter and chocolate stains on my hands.'

'How did she get into the house without leaving a trace? Did she already have a copy of Aleesha's key cut in preparation to get revenge on her?'

'No. It turns out that she's very handy with a lock-picking tool. Something about dominatrix dungeons, handcuffs, and kinky role-playing.'

I scrunched up my face. 'Don't say any more. I'm getting a really horrible picture in my head. How did she know the alarm code, though?'

'Aleesha must've had a hard time remembering it because it was changed so often. She stored it under her contacts on her mobile phone. Before Jessie confronted Steve about him and Aleesha, she was suspicious they were having an affair. So Jessie went through Aleesha's phone one day when it was lying around on set, looking for texts between the two of them. She stumbled across Aleesha's alarm code and memorized it before she planned how she was going to get her back for ruining her career and her love life.'

They say a mobile phone could save your life one day, but I bet they don't say it can kill you, too. 'If Aleesha stored the code under a fake number in her phone, how did Jessie guess it was the alarm code?'

'That's just it. Aleesha had the code listed under "Alarm".' Brad shook his head.

Well, don't try that at home, folks!

He took my hand in his. 'Hell hath no fury like a woman scorned.'

I squeezed Brad's hand. He squeezed it back.

'Shh, don't talk now. You need to get some rest,' he said.

'What about Vegas?' I said softly, feeling myself drifting off.

'The doctor says you can't travel for a while, but Vegas will still be waiting for us as soon as you're better. We'll just change the flights.'

'At this rate Tia and Hacker will get married before us.' I slipped into la-la land, dreaming Brad was standing at the end of the aisle as Elvis belted out 'Love me Tender'. I dreamed of the vows I'd written for the wedding, the sexy Fandango dress clinging to me, the softness of Brad's lips on mine and the hardness of his body pressed into me as we rolled around in our bed on the wedding night.

Nope. I was definitely not nun material.

Next stop, Vegas!

Chocolate, Lies, and Murder
Sibel Hodge

Copyright © Sibel Hodge 2013

The moral right of the author has been asserted. All rights reserved in all media. No part of this book may be reproduced or transmitted in any form by any means, electronic or mechanical (including but not limited to: the Internet, photocopying, recording or by any information storage and retrieval system), without prior permission in writing from the author and/or publisher.

This is a work of fiction. Names, characters, places, brands, media, and incidents are either the product of the author's imagination or are used fictitiously. The author acknowledges the trademarked status and trademark owners of various products referenced in this work of fiction, which have been used without permission. The publication/use of these trademarks is not authorized, associated with, or sponsored by the trademark owners.

This book is licensed for your personal enjoyment only. This book may not be re-sold or given away to other people. If you would like to share this book with another person, please purchase an additional copy for each person you share it with. If you're reading this book and did not purchase it, or it was not purchased for your use only, then you should return to your online retailer and purchase your own copy. Thank you for respecting the author's work.

Printed in Great Britain
by Amazon.co.uk, Ltd.,
Marston Gate.